ROMANCE AND RACE
VIBERT MILLER

This book is a work of fiction. All characters, names, places and incidents appearing in this work are products of the author's imagination. Any resemblance to real persons, living or dead, is entirely coincidental.

Table of Contents

CHAPTER ONE 1

CHAPTER TWO 5

CHAPTER THREE 9

CHAPTER FOUR 15

CHAPTER FIVE 20

CHAPTER SIX 24

CHAPTER SEVEN 30

CHAPTER EIGHT 34

CHAPTER NINE 40

CHAPTER TEN 44

CHAPTER ELEVEN 49

CHAPTER TWELVE 52

CHAPTER THIRTEEN 55

CHAPTER FOURTEEN 59

CHAPTER FIFTEEN 63

CHAPTER SIXTEEN 67

CHAPTER SEVENTEEN 70

CHAPTER EIGHTEEN 72

CHAPTER NINETEEN 76

CHAPTER TWENTY 80

CHAPTER TWENTY-ONE 83

CHAPTER TWENTY-TWO 88

CHAPTER TWENTY-THREE 91

CHAPTER TWENTY-FOUR 95

CHAPTER TWENTY-FIVE 100

CHAPTER TWENTY-SIX 105

CHAPTER ONE

"I don't date black men," that is what Amelia Knight hurled at Derek Roberts when he invited her for a cup of coffee, at the café across the street from their condo building.

"Sorry if I offended you, but the fact is I don't date black men. There, I said it."

Derek searched for a comeback but came up empty. He finally retorted, "I wasn't asking for a date. Besides I am not black. If you look carefully you will see I am brown."

Amy screwed up her face and answered, "you're joking, right? You're pulling my leg."

"Hell, no. I wouldn't pull your leg for a million pesos."

"Why? What's wrong with my legs?"

"Nothing. I saw them when you were moving in. You were wearing shorts and they looked great. The trouble is they are white with blonde fuzz all over them. I'm grabbing this taxi. Bye."

Before Amelia could respond that she does not usually walk around with hairy legs, the taxi took off with him.

Amelia was a senior accountant in an accounting firm. She had just turned forty, was not married, was not dating anyone seriously and was beginning to feel life was passing her by. That remark about her hairy legs rankled her. She wondered if Derek, was that his name? just said that because she had turned him down. It was true that the days leading up to her move were chaotic and she may have let herself slip a little and maybe her legs showed a little fuzz, but they were definitely not hairy. At any rate she could do something about her legs but there was nothing he could do about being black or brown as he said.

She had just sat down behind her desk when another accountant sauntered into her office. Her friend, Anna, took one look at her and knew something was wrong.

"What's happening? You look like you swallowed a knife."

"I had a run in with my neighbor and he ticked me off. He said my legs are hairy."

"Oh boy," Anna said, "knowing how much time you spend making sure you look good, that is the final insult. What brought that on?"

"I told him I won't go out with him."

"Why won't you? Does he have two heads or something?"

"No. Actually he is a fine-looking man. Tall, handsome, nice teeth, full head of hair. But he is black. Well, brown."

"What? I can't believe you just said that. Amy, you do know I'm Hispanic."

"I know that," Amy replied, "but this is different."

"How so?"

"I don't know, but I think it is. I have to think about this."

Derek Roberts was in a taxi heading to the office of his literary agent. The agent had asked him to stop by to go over a contract the publisher had sent him for Derek's newest book. Roberts was a best-selling author writing crime thrillers under the pseudonym D.R. Fisher. His mind was on the conversation he had with his new neighbor Amelia. He had never encountered anyone so blatantly rude. He could not bring himself to believe she was racist but to say she did not date black men without following up with a good reason certainly led one to that conclusion. Of course, she had a right to refuse to date anybody she wanted. Hell, it was not even a date just two neighbors having a cup of coffee and getting to know one another. His agent picked up on the vibes he was throwing off as soon as he walked in the door. When

Derek relayed his earlier conversation the agent's response was, "forget about her. She is not worth your time."

That was true but it still angered him. In addition to the contract they were discussing, the agent presented Derek with a large check from another publisher for another one of his best-sellers. This mollified him a little so that by the time he arrived back home he was able to put Amy out of his mind. Later that afternoon he decided to go out to dinner and just as he approached the elevator the door opened and Amy stepped out. They both raised a hand in greeting at the same time.

"Am I allowed to say hello when I see you?" he asked.

"Of course. And I apologize for earlier. That was tasteless of me."

"No problem. I get it." As he stood talking to her the elevator door closed and it left.

"Sorry. You missed the elevator."

"That's okay it will come back. I was not aware the elderly couple who owned your apartment had put it on the market."

"They still own it. I am just renting. I imagine you're renting too." Amy said.

"No. I own my place," Derek said.

"You own it? I am surprised. I know what these apartments go for and I didn't think..."

"I could afford to buy one" Derek supplied. "You're probably wondering how big my welfare check is."

"I didn't say that. Don't put words in my mouth. But since you mentioned it how can you afford a place like this?"

"Okay, I'll tell you but you have to promise not to tell anyone. I am in a special welfare program that gives me all the money I need for anything." Amy was staring at Derek as he spoke trying to absorb what he was telling her.

"If you're not putting me on, tell me about this special program you're in."

"I'm not going to tell you because you will want to get in on it. The welfare people won't like that. Here's the elevator. Bye."

Derek had a smug smile on his face as he rode down. He was proud of himself for having hit back at her. That's it he thought. Every time he ran into her he was going to feed her more of such stereotypical crap and watch her deal with it. Of course, she would try to get information about the program and when she realized she'd been had, the egg would be on her face.

CHAPTER TWO

A week had passed since Derek's meeting with Amy. It was poker night at his place and they were a little noisy. Put six men together with beer, pizza and cards and you have a noisy crowd. It sounded as if someone had sat on Derek's doorbell and one of the guys opened the door and saw Amy standing there.

"Who ordered the stripper?" he yelled out, turning Amy's face red.

"What does she look like?" Derek asked, "is she a tall blonde with a great body?"

"Yep that's her. Pretty too."

"Oh, that's my neighbor. Ignore her. Hold on. She doesn't date black men so that leaves me out. But you're white ask her for a date."

"What about me?" asked the only Chinese man in the group.

"I don't know, Lee. She hasn't voiced an opinion on Asians."

Amy pushed her way into the apartment and stood with her arms akimbo. "I didn't come here to be insulted," she barked. "You're making too much noise and I want you to consider your neighbors."

"Boy, is she steamed," one of the men said.

"And a looker too," another added.

"Okay, Amy," Derek said, "we'll keep it down. We're just about done here anyway"

"No, we're not," the one who answered the door said, "you cleaned us out. You have to give us a chance to get some of our money back." He looked at Amy. "You should date him and order the most expensive item on the menu." Amy turned on her heels and left the apartment. She briefly wondered if she should alert the authorities that Derek was gambling away his welfare money. She was convinced that was his source of income since she had never seen him leaving for work and he was home all day. Either that or he was into drugs. The furnishings in his apartment shouted money. In less than half an hour Derek's apartment was silent.

Her brief encounter with Derek's friends had left Amy shaken. She discounted his pronouncement that he was in a special welfare program. No welfare program, no matter how special, would pay for that apartment and the furnishings. That left drugs. She knew from news reports that there was a lot of money in drugs. Didn't she read somewhere that most drug runners were black? If Derek was involved in drugs then he was a dangerous man. And living next door to him scared her.

A month later she was coming home from work just as Derek was leaving. He held the door open for her and she forced a smile. "Thanks for keeping the noise down that night" she said.

"Don't think of it," Derek answered, "always ready to help a neighbor. By the way don't be alarmed if you see people coming to my place at odd hours. It's just business. Goodnight."

Amy stared after him as he stood outside waiting for a taxi. She couldn't see the smile that played on his face. Another stereotype covered.

Derek had just settled down to watch a football game when he heard his doorbell followed by knocking. Someone was anxious to speak to him. It was Amy.

"Hello Amy. You look panicked. What's going on?"

"Can you help me? I think there is someone in my apartment."

"Did you call the police?"

"No. I am not really sure. I just saw a shadow and if it turns out to be nothing the police won't like that."

"So, you want me to do what?"

"Maybe you can ring the bell and see if anybody comes out."

"Okay, let's go."

"Aren't you going to get your gun?" she asked.

"My gun? I don't have a gun." he said.

"But I thought all…"

"I know all black men have guns," he smiled when her face paled. "Come on, stand back I'm going to ring the bell and see what happens." He pushed the button and they could hear the doorbell. The door opened and out stepped a man dressed in a suit.

"Joe," Amy shouted, "what are you doing here? How did you get into my apartment? Derek this is my ex-boyfriend whom I broke up with two months ago. You haven't answered. How did you get in here?"

"I still have a key. I was waiting for you so we could talk."

"There is nothing to talk about. Give me my key and just in case you've made a copy, I am having the lock changed tomorrow."

"No need," Joe said, "this is the only key." She had her hand out for the key.

"You don't need me," Derek said, "I'll go back to my game." He left them in front of Amy's apartment. He turned in their direction in time to see Joe entering the elevator just as Amy closed her door. The gun. She actually thought he had a gun. Given all her beliefs he could understand why she did not want to date black men.

Amy was putting the finishing touches to her dinner when she heard voices coming from the front of her apartment. She hurried to the door and looked through the security peephole in time to see Derek with a woman. She had never seen him with a woman before, so she was curious. She opened her door and pretended to be going to the elevator but she and Derek made eye contact.

"Oh, hello Derek," she said.

"Hi Amy. Come and meet Spring Flower," Derek said.

"Spring Flower. Is that a Native American name?"

"No," Spring spoke up, "it is Indian."

"But I thought Indian and Native American are one and…"

"This calls for an explanation," Derek interrupted, "Spring, may I?"

"Of course. She is your friend."

Derek thought 'friend' might not be the appropriate word but it would do for now. "Spring is from the Chippewa Nation. Her ancestors occupied the North Dakota area. She believes for hundreds maybe thousands of years they were known as Indians. Now comes the white man who tells them they should be called Native Americans. She doesn't like it. And I don't blame her."

Amy was a little flustered when she heard this, and all she could get out was, "I see. Er, how did you meet?"

"Spring is an attorney. Her firm is doing some legal work for the company I work for and she drew the short straw. I met her when she came to the office the day I was there."

Spring was a beautiful young woman with skin the color of coffee with milk and glistening jet black hair that hung to her shoulders.

"I'm taking Spring to dinner at a restaurant near here and she wanted to see my apartment especially my shell collection. Come in and have a drink with us, that is if that is not against the rules."

"I would be glad to have a drink," Amy said, "I didn't know you had a shell collection."

"Then it would be a surprise."

While Spring was in the bathroom Amy took the opportunity to pry. "I don't mean to pry," she said, "but is Spring your girlfriend?"

"No. Not at all," Derek replied, "she's too young for me. She is planning to go back to North Dakota once she's had some legal experience under her belt. She expects to spend about two years here in Chicago."

Spring came out of the bathroom and nodded to Derek. "Ready whenever you are."

Derek stood and they said goodbye to Amy.

CHAPTER THREE

Amy was convinced Derek was an enigma that defied understanding. At least to her. He had told her not to be alarmed when she saw people coming to him at odd hours, but three months later no one had come. Of course, they could have been coming in droves while she was at work, but somehow she didn't think so. He said he had a job with a company where he met Spring but so far she had never seen him leave for work. He seemed to have no visible means of income yet he lived in a lavishly furnished apartment and with an extensive shell collection no less. Amy had many questions about Derek but the one question she avoided was why was she so interested in her neighbor. He, mostly, ignored her and kept to himself. Basically, he was a good neighbor and never bothered her. One Saturday afternoon she was about to leave her building when a taxi drove up. She could see Derek getting ready to exit the taxi so she pulled back into a corner, whipped out her cell and took a picture of him just as he turned to enter the building. They greeted each other in passing as usual. Monday morning, she showed the picture to Anna in her office. Anna declared him a hunk.

"What's your obsession with this man?" Anna wanted to know.

"I don't know. Do you think I'm obsessed?"

"I would say, yes. You already told him you won't go out with him. Seems to me he accepted that and is not bothering you. So, why?"

Amy could not answer that and a week later it became even more complicated. The building they lived in had an underground garage for owners. Amy did not have a car and she didn't know Derek had one since he was always in a taxi. The entrance to the garage was a short distance from the front door. Amy was leaving and stepped into the street to hail a taxi when a vintage Rolls Royce came out of the garage. The beautiful car caught her attention and she almost dropped her purse when she saw Derek behind the wheel. Amy did not know much about cars but she knew this one. She saw one like it in a movie. It was a Rolls Royce Silver Cloud, and Derek was driving it. She knew she had to find out how he could afford a Rolls Royce. She got an opportunity just three days later in the elevator. She asked if it was him driving a Rolls Royce.

"Yeah," he said, "that was me. She's a beauty isn't she? It was a labor of love for me."

"What do you mean?" she asked.

"I saw it abandoned in a garage and made a deal with the owner to buy it for almost nothing. It was in terrible shape but the body was still sound. I bought it, rented garage space and went to work bringing it back to life. I took shop in high school and learned my way around cars. It took me three years because I could only work on it part-time. So, what you saw is the result of a lot of labor and time scrounging for parts."

"You look good in it, by the way," Amy said.

"Well, I'll be damned," Derek responded, "a compliment. Thank you."

The elevator stopped at their floor and they went to their separate doors.

"See you later, Amy,"

"You too, Derek."

A few nights later Amy's doorbell rang and she opened her door to find Derek there.

"I just want to tell you it's my turn to host poker night, but we'll try to keep it down."

"Oh, thanks for telling me. What kind of poker do you play?"

"Texas hold 'em. Do you play?"

"Oh no. My father did. How many of you will there be?"

"The usual six. We take turns hosting."

Amy had an idea. She kept listening for the men's arrivals while making sandwiches. She knew they usually ordered in pizza so she had to spring her surprise before they ordered.

She went to Derek's door with a large basket loaded with an assortment of sandwiches. The surprise on Derek's face was worth every ounce of the effort she had made. He had only one word.

"Why?" he asked.

"Just being neighborly," she said.

Derek yelled out, "Tom, cancel the pizza. Amy has brought us a ton of sandwiches."

All the men got up and took her by the hand and brought her into the apartment. One of them told her to sit in on the game. They would teach her and go easy on her. But she couldn't bear to see her money disappearing, so she declined. Derek walked her to the door and thanked her again and offered his help anytime she needed it.

Amy sat in her comfortable armchair with a book and thought if Derek was a drug pusher, he was the gentlest one on the planet. It did not add up. It bothered her that she could not reconcile his lifestyle with his lack of a job. It all came back to drugs and she was ready to accept that. There had to be a way to resolve this and her company offered it. She found out the man who ran the mailroom was retiring and they needed someone new. She told Derek about it. He said nothing for a long time and she thought she had insulted him. At last, he smiled and thanked her for thinking of him but he had to tell her he was sure he could do better than being a mailroom clerk. He decided to level with her, sort of.

"I know you are confused about my job situation. Here I am living in a luxurious apartment, driving an expensive car, dining out several times a week, all with no visible means of an income."

He stopped to allow her time to absorb what he had said and maybe give an answer.

"Well, it's none of my business," she said.

"True," he said, "but you wondered. And I bet you think I'm dealing drugs."

"Well I.."

"No. No need to answer that. Here are the facts. I am not a drug dealer. The money to buy this apartment and maintain my lifestyle came from a source you may one day learn about. I am not ready to divulge that but I can assure you it is totally legit. Let me tell you about my friends I play poker with. They are all respectable men. Lee, the Asian, works in the Chinese Consulate office here in Chicago. Tom is an attorney in his own firm, Jack is the CFO of a software company. As you see we are a little United Nations. Black, brown and white."

Amy wanted answers and she got them. But instead of feeling successful, she felt like a total failure. How could she have allowed society to cloud her intelligence. The only words that came to her were, "I'm sorry."

Amy had not seen Derek for about two weeks. She rang his doorbell several times but he was not home. Then one evening the elevator door opened and he stepped out. They greeted each other and Amy told him she had rung his bell a couple of times. He told her he had gone away for two weeks.

"Vacation?" she said.

"Yeah and a little business too." Her eyes betrayed her.

"No, Amy, it wasn't drug business. This is something entirely different. One day I will tell you about it. For now, you have to be content with what I have told you."

She still had his picture on her phone and she brought it up to look at it. Her friend had said he was a hunk. Judging from his height, his shoulders, his flat belly and his chiseled features she had to admit her friend was correct. She judged him to be in his mid-forties, four or five years older than she was. It was six months since she made that announcement that she had no interest in dating a black man. He never invited her again. Not even for coffee, but he was warm and friendly with her. She was not sure she wanted their relationship to go further, but she knew if she did she would have to make the first move. She decided on a trial run. If things did not go well she could always back out.

Amy rang Derek's doorbell. She heard him yell, "coming" and the door opened. He was dressed to go out.

"Looks like I caught you at the wrong time. You're going out."

"Just to dinner," he said, "what's up?"

"I stopped by to invite you to dinner at my place next Saturday," she said.

A frown crossed his face and it looked as if he were making up his mind about something. "Sorry, I can't accept," he said, "you see, I don't accept dinner invitations from white women."

This knocked Amy back. She looked at his face and there were no smiles there. The man was serious.

"Are you serious?" she asked.

"Very. Rumor has it a white woman would break your heart in a minute. It starts out as an innocent dinner invitation and next thing the poor black man is caught up in a web and then he is done for."

"Where did you hear such nonsense?"

"Oh, it's common knowledge around the neighborhood." They stared at each other, dark clouds rippling across their faces. Derek broke first.

"Of course, it's nonsense." The clouds vanished and left a broad smile on his face. "I would be delighted to come to your place for dinner. What can I bring?"

"Just yourself. Boy you almost gave me a heart attack. Go enjoy your dinner. See you on Saturday."

"What are we having?"

"It's a surprise. Come hungry."

CHAPTER FOUR

Friday evening Derek and Amy arrived at their building at the same time. She was carrying a bag of groceries and he had a book in his hand. She glanced at the cover and noted the author.

"You read D.R. Fisher too," she said, "He is my favorite, but I have not read this one."

"It just came out."

"In that case the library won't have it yet."

"Library, eh. You don't buy them?"

"Why should I. The library carries all his books. They usual buy two copies and that means I will have to wait my turn but he is worth the wait."

"Tell you what. You can borrow mine when I'm finished with it."

Saturday evening Derek showed up at Amy's dressed for an upscale restaurant and carrying two bottles of wine. He brought one bottle of red and one of white. She did not tell him what was on the menu so he wanted to cover all bases. She thanked him and told him to take off his jacket and loosen his tie.

"What about my shoes?" he asked, "shall I keep them on?"

"You shall, yes." He told her he would be right back, he forgot something. He came back with a package and offered it to her.

"What's this?"

"Open it. I think you will like it." She tore open the wrapping paper and found the book by D.R. Fisher.

"You're trying to make me feel like a cheapie," she said.

"Not at all," he said, "I'm trying to make Fisher richer."

"Don't bother, the man is loaded. Not only are his books best sellers but two of them have been made into movies. And you know how much movie producers pay for good books."

"A lot?"

"You better believe it."

Dinner was a delight. The lobsters were cooked to perfection and Derek remarked on them and asked her, jokingly, if she had them flown in from Maine. She said she did not but the store where she bought them did.

"I have something to tell you," Amy said, "anytime now I'm going to spin my white woman web and ensnare you. You should have paid attention to the rumors."

"That's okay, spin away. I have immunity and I have something to tell you. I wouldn't mind being ensnared by you."

Amy stopped what she was doing and stared at him. "Derek, what are you saying?"

"I have no idea. I think that was the wine talking." Amy said nothing, but got busy putting stuff away.. She needed to keep her hands busy so she can fully comprehend what Derek was implying. He on the other hand decided to make a joke out of it. "I feel my immunity slipping. That web you're spinning is closing in on me. Maybe I should make my escape now." He stood and slung his jacket over his shoulder. Before she knew what was happening he drew her in and hugged her. This was the first time he had ever touched her and she smelled his aftershave. She did not hug him back because she had no idea what she wanted to do. He whispered in her hair that she was a fantastic cook and he had a wonderful time. Then he let her go and slipped out her door.

"I had a wonderful time too," she said. It was said so softly, she did not think he heard her

Amy knew her relationship with Derek had moved to a new level and she was not ready for it. She also knew the time was approaching when he would ask her out and she had to prepare herself for this. His race had fallen into the background. She might even consider herself something of trail blazer, although interracial dating and marriage were no longer despicable activities. The huge elephant in the room was the fact he was a slacker. She thought of him as a slacker because he had no solid employment. Pushing drugs was not gainful employment, no matter how much money was made. She had just found a reason to refuse his invitation. The problem, however, was that he never invited her

A month passed and their relationship was still at the 'hello, how are you' stage. What was wrong with Derek? Why couldn't he man up and ask her for a date, her reasoning went. She had him over for dinner he could at least reciprocate. That would be the neighborly thing to do.

One day after their hello at the elevator he did it. He asked her over for dinner.

"It's time I do the neighborly thing," he said. "What are your feelings about coming to my place for dinner. Can you put aside the black and white thing?"

"Obviously I have no qualms about putting that aside. I had you over. Remember?"

"I do remember and it was great. However, I must warn you I am not a good cook but I am great at ordering. How about next Saturday evening? And no, I am not telling what we're having. It will be a surprise."

"Okay," Amy said, "it's a date."

"A date?"

"Well not a date, date. You know what I mean."

Dinner at Derek's was almost a repeat of the earlier dinner at Amy's with one notable exception. It was catered.

Amy arrived to find the dining table opened to its fullest to seat eight people even though it was only the two of them. But what knocked her back was the lady in the kitchen who was preparing the meal. It was duck cooked in the French style. Derek introduced her as Mrs. LaBonte. She was Haitian now living in the US and her business was catering dinner parties, only she did it at the client's home.

"I never knew this was possible," Amy said afterwards, "but a great idea."

"Yeah. She does a good business. Tonight, was only the two of us so she was alone, but I've been to dinner parties with more guests. In those cases, she brings in more staff including her son who serves drinks and her two daughters who act as servers. Quite a few friends use her. Did you enjoy the duck?"

"The best I ever had, not that I am any expert. It was delicious. I don't want to seem tactless, but she must come at a high price."

"Sort of, but worth it. You wouldn't have enjoyed what I cook. I got the idea from one of my friends."

Derek was now a total mystery to Amy. She'd never heard of a drug lord who had the social grace to cater a dinner for his date. Not that this was a date, but nobody had ever done that for her.

If his goal was to impress her, he achieved it in abundance. Mrs. LaBonte cleaned up and left after Derek thanked her for the fantastic meal and she thanked him for the business. She even smiled at Amy as she left.

"Would you like an after dinner drink?" Derek asked.

"Sure." He went to a highly polished cabinet and brought out a bottle of cognac and two glasses. Amy could not help noticing the cognac was one of the most expensive. The evening wound down and soon Amy was thanking him and saying goodbye. She expected him to hug her but he did not. He just squeezed her arm and thanked her for coming. She had barely entered her apartment when the idea exploded in her head. The man was gay. She had put on the sexiest dress she owned and it did not faze him. He did not even attempt a pass. She had never heard of a gay drug pusher but why not, there are many things she did not know about the world of drugs. She did know one gay man.

She made a mental note to ask him if he knew of any gay men involved in pushing drugs and made a lot of money doing it.

CHAPTER FIVE

Derek was enjoying himself at Amy's expense. A man with no visible income to speak of, living in an expensive apartment, driving a Rolls Royce and hiring a caterer for a dinner date. Confusion must be running rampant in her head. He was going to let her off the hook soon but he wanted to have a little more fun with her. But he was bothered about what he was doing because he had felt something for her the first time he invited her for coffee and that feeling was getting stronger. Every time he saw her he had to struggle to keep from kissing her. Maybe she would slap him but it would be worth it. Amy had no idea what she was doing to him. A new thought occurred to him. The time had come for action. He was going to ring her doorbell and march right into her apartment and ask her out. He needed to know how strongly she felt about not dating a black man.

They were standing staring at each other after the question. He could almost hear the gears in her head and she probably heard his.

"What made you decide to ask me out?" she said.

"I thought that since we had dinners at each other's apartment we might make a bold move and go out into the world."

"I think you're poking fun at me," she said.

"I am not. I would love to take you out and I needed to know how committed you are to what you said."

"I am no longer committed to all that stupidity, thanks to you. You've opened my eyes. There is one thing, however, I cannot skip over."

"Only one? That's progress. What is it?"

This was the day Amy dreaded for a long time. She was about to confront Derek about being lazy and without ambition.

"I really don't know how to say it, because, it's none of my business,"

"Don't let that stop you, Amy," Derek said, "you've been straightforward so far, why stop now?"

"I can't abide anyone just drifting through life. I know you came into some money but you're still an able-bodied man. You should have a job. I just don't see myself spending time with a man who is just taking up space."

"What about drug running? Isn't that a job?"

Amy's eyes were about to pop out of her head. "Are you a drug runner?"

"No, Amy. I already told you I am not. Let's end this conversation this way. I'll get a job that you can see, and I'll show you my first paycheck. Hold off on your decision about going out with me until then. Could you accept that?"

"That seems fair. Okay, I accept."

Derek headed for the door and he was almost through when he added, "we'll go back to 'hi, how are you' until we resolve this conundrum."

She was left staring at the closed door. That was not what she had in mind but she had no argument against it. There was something else gnawing at her. She had known Derek for about six months and in that time she had not gone out on a single date. She always found good reasons to refuse. Now, she was wondering if he had gone on dates.

They met at their usual place in front of the elevator. "Hi Amy," he said, "how are you? Got to run. I'm job hunting."

"Hey, wait a minute," Amy said, "you don't have to rush off like that."

"Of course, I have to. I'm job hunting. Is that mailroom job still open at your office?"

"Come on, Derek," she said, "you don't want to be a mailroom clerk. Besides the position has been filled."

"Darn. Well, if anything comes up let me know." They reached the ground floor and exited the building. Derek saw a taxi and hailed it.

A taxi? He's taking a taxi? Who goes job hunting in a taxi?

Two weeks later, Derek had still not found a job. He saw Amy and she asked him about it. "Any luck?" she asked.

"Not yet," he replied, "well maybe I might get something. You know I work sometimes for a company doing research using my computer at home. It doesn't pay much and it is not steady. That's why I haven't said anything about it."

"I think you mentioned it in passing."

"I did? Well, they're offering me a full-time position in house. The problem is the job is in San Francisco. I can move, of course, but I like living in Chicago. Hate the winters but the summers are great."

"You mean if you take the job you'll have to move away?"

"Yeah. Out to the west coast."

"Are you going to take it?" there was anxiety in Amy's voice.

"I haven't decided yet. What do you think I should do?"

"Oh, I, um, it's your decision."

"The good thing about that," he said, "takes the burden off you."

"The burden? What are you talking about?"

"You won't have to decide about going out with me." Derek said.

"I don't see that as a burden," Amy said.

They had not run into one another for three weeks and Amy became very anxious that Derek had taken the job and moved away. And he did not say goodbye. Her doorbell rang and she hurried to open it. It was Derek and he was smiling broadly. And for the first time his greeting was a hug.

"It's show and tell time." He said. "You said if I got a job and showed you my paycheck you would go out with me. I'm holding you to that."

"First, tell me what the job is," Amy said.

"It is with a literary agency. Here is the check I received today. He handed a check to her, made out for the sum of three hundred and fifty thousand dollars" She looked at the check and then at him and back at the check. She was rendered speechless.

"Where is the book I gave you? Please bring it," Derek said. She gave it to him without comment.

Derek held up the book. "D.R. Fisher is a pen name. This guy's real name is Derek Reginald Roberts. My name. This check is the last payment for one of my books that became a movie"

Amy slumped into the nearest chair still speechless.

"So, you see, Amy," Derek said, "I do have a job, and good paying one at that."

"My God," she finally found her voice, "you were lying to me."

"Not exactly. I may have stretched the truth and left out some things."

"You told me you came into some money when you bought your apartment."

"That was not a lie. I came into money when I sold my book to the movie company."

"So, all the time I was going on about how much I like reading D.R. Fisher, I was telling you how much I like reading you."

"Yes. And it felt good. Now that I have a good paying job will you let me take you out?"

"If you think I'm going to say no to my favorite author, you're crazy. Of course, I will go out with you."

CHAPTER SIX

The restaurant Derek took Amy to was reputed to be the best in Chicago. The owner, a Frenchman who claimed he lost his way out to the west coast and ended up in Chicago, also claimed his restaurant was American with a French flavor. It was rumored that guests crossed the pond and then the lake to come to his restaurant, though this was just a rumor. Reservations to dine there required a guest to be put on a waiting list and wait weeks, unless he knew the owner personally. Derek did. How he came to be acquainted with Monsieur Jacques Trevant was a story both he and Jacques preferred to remain buried. But Derek had done the Frenchman a big favor. As a younger man Jacques was quite a playboy even though he was married. Derek was staying in a hotel in Cannes on the French Riviera doing research for a book. Early one evening he was leaving his room when a man came barreling down the corridor dressed only in his underwear. The man stopped Derek and begged him to allow him to enter his room. It seems the husband of the woman he was with was after him holding a gun. Derek felt sorry for the man and pulled him into the room and closed the door. Through the security hole he saw the husband pass by and indeed he had a gun.

Derek allowed the man to stay for most of the evening. He, originally, was on his way to dinner but they ordered up from room service including champagne and had a fabulous time. The Frenchman was very grateful to Derek claiming he saved his life. He told Derek he was a chef and in a few weeks he was emigrating to the US where he planned to open a restaurant. When Derek asked him where he was headed he said probably San Francisco but he was not sure. Derek then told him about Chicago. Why not come to Chicago? Jacques Trevant ended up in Chicago, fell in love with the city on the lake and eventually was the owner of the finest restaurant in the area. And Derek was always a VIP. Whenever he wanted to dine there he called Jacques personally and the owner always made room for him. Also, Jacques was one of two people who knew Derek was the celebrated D.R. Fisher. His agent was the other and now Amelia Knight was the third.

After they were seated, Amy looked around in awe of the ambiance of the restaurant. They were at a table that looked out over Lake Michigan, with glasses of champagne in their hands, compliments of the house.

"I have been told reservations to this restaurant are hard to come by," Amy said, " you have to wait weeks. How did you manage it?"

"I know the owner," Derek said with a smile.

"No. Really. How did you do it?"

"I know the owner," Derek insisted and proceeded to tell her the story of saving Jacques's life in France.. "Here comes Jacques now." Amy looked up and a round man who looked like he enjoyed his own cooking too much, was approaching their table. Derek stood and the two encircled each other.

"Ah, D.R. I mean Derek, it's been too long."

"How are you Jacques? Meet my friend, Amelia." Amy put out her hand and Jacques raised it to his lips.

"Enchante," he said, still the charmer. Then he looked at Derek and winked. He approved of Amy.

"He knows you are Fisher, I take it," Amy said.

"He does. In adding up the people who know, I forgot him."

"You know, your secret is slowly leaking out."

"Yeah. But forget about that let's allow Jacques's exquisite cooking to enchant us."

Derek had taken Amy to dinner in his Rolls Royce and she had to admit she totally enjoyed the envy of the people who were waiting for their cars, when the Rolls arrived and the attendant handed her into it. Back home, they stood at her apartment door. Neither one seemed to know what move to make. Amy had already told him many times, how much she enjoyed the evening and she felt like royalty. It was time to move on. She was surprised to hear herself saying "would you like to come in for coffee or something stronger?"

Derek seemed to be waiting for that because he took her hand while he opened the door, and when inside, put his arms around her and kissed her deeply. To the surprise of both of them, Amy responded with the same eagerness. She, too, was waiting for this moment. She led him to her sofa and went into the kitchen to get drinks.

"I don't have cognac," she said, "would sherry do?"

"Sherry would be excellent," Derek replied.

She sat very close to him on the sofa. They each took a sip, put down their glasses and was in each other's arms again and again, the kisses getting deeper and deeper until they were breathless.

"An observation, if I may," Derek said.

"You may."

"For a white woman who doesn't date black men, you certainly have a strange way of showing it," Derek said.

"And for a black man who doesn't accept invitations from white women, you certainly have a strange way of responding," Amy said.

They exhausted themselves with the kissing then Derek got up slowly and reluctantly left.

Derek had just finished a chapter in the novel he was writing and had adjourned to the living room to find a movie on television when there was a banging on the wall between his living room and Amy's. Sounds like she's moving furniture he thought. She should have asked for his help because it sounded like heavy stuff. The banging came again louder and longer. This wasn't furniture he realized. Something was wrong. He hurried over to Amy's door and he could see through a gap in the drapes, a man had Amy pinned to the wall with his hand around her throat. He dialed 911, told the operator what was happening and where and she should tell the police to hurry. Then he stepped back and with all his strength he blasted the door. The lock broke loose and he stumbled into the apartment. He righted himself and grabbed the man by his hair and yanked back as hard as he could. The man let Amy go and turned into Derek's fist which connected with his jaw. Derek heard bones breaking and watched the man go down. But he managed to raise himself but he didn't get far because Derek's fist pummeled into his rib cage. This time he stayed down.

Derek went over to Amy who was shaking. Two police officers rushed into the apartment with guns drawn and demanding what the hell was going on. Derek told them. Derek did not get a good look at the man as he was hitting him and he was lying on the floor with his face turned away, so he was surprised when Amy told the cop she knew the man. He was her ex-boyfriend.

Amy was against the wall with her dress torn off and her underwear askew. The man was definitely in the process of sexually assaulting her. It turned out she had let him in because he claimed he just wanted a minute to talk to her, but turned violent when she refused his advances. By this time the ambulance that was called, arrived.

The police told them they were recording everything on their body cameras. Amy told them she didn't want to appear on camera in just her underwear but they convinced her it was in her best interest to show what had taken place. They were going to charge the man with attempted sexual battery and attempted murder since he was choking her.

"It is not *attempted* sexual battery. It was sexual battery because he squeezed my breasts and had put his hand in my underpants. When I fought him off he started to choke me. That's when I started banging on the wall hoping Derek was at home."

"You say you know the man," one cop said.

"Yes. We used to date but I broke it off several months ago. He came here tonight and said he just wanted to talk. I shouldn't have let him in but I did."

"And you, sir," the cop turned to Derek, "can I have your name and tell us how you came to be here. Looks like you may have saved this woman from being sexually assaulted and maybe, even losing her life."

"I heard her banging on the wall and knew something was wrong. I looked through that gap in the drapes and saw he had her up against the wall with his hands around her throat. I broke down the door and punched him twice. The rest you know."

One of the police officers examined the broken lock. "This lock is torn off. What are you a football player?"

"Used to. In college. Tackle."

"The NFL know about you?"

"Yeah. After college," Derek said, "I went in a different direction. I'm too old now anyway."

As the medics took Joe away one of them said, "this guy is gonna be in a lot of hurt. He has a broken jaw and maybe a couple of ribs too."

One of the officers asked Derek, "would you be willing to testify in court about your part in this?"

"Damn straight," Derek said.

"And you ma'am are you willing to testify?"

"Damn straight."

"Um, a simple 'yes' would be better." The cop said.

"Okay, yes," Derek answered.

"And you?" he was looking at Amy.

"Yes," she replied.

Before they left they advised Amy to find a room in a hotel or with a friend since her door was broken. She asked Derek if he would give her a ride to a hotel. He said no but he could give her a guest room for the night or however long it took to fix her door.

The next morning, Amy went into the kitchen to find Derek sitting at the table with a notebook and a cup of coffee.

"What are you reading?" she asked.

"Going over some notes. Working," he replied. "Coffee? Or I can make breakfast."

"Let me," she said, "not that I don't trust your cooking. I called in sick."

"Good idea on both. You went through a traumatizing experience last night. Calling in sick today is to be expected. I'm thinking you should consult an attorney to get a judge to place a restraining order on that man so that if he comes within a hundred feet of you, he would be liable to arrest. And this is after he spends some time in prison."

"I don't know any attorneys," Amy said.

"That's where I come in handy. One of my poker buddies is an attorney."

You come in handy in many ways, she thought but did not say.

CHAPTER SEVEN

Fall had arrived in Chicago. The days were still warm with a nice breeze coming in off the lake, but the nights were turning into sweater weather. Derek asked Amy if she had vacation time coming and she explained she had two weeks coming which she could take at any time except between January and April. Tax time. Why was he asking?

"The movie studio plans to start shooting my book in January and they invited me to come out to the coast, to get together with the couple they hired to write the screenplay. I am inviting you to come with me. I'm thinking two weeks in November. Just when that cold wind starts howling off the lake."

"Really? I would be delighted. I'll put in for it immediately." Amy said.

"Did I mention it's all expenses paid?"

"We still have some nice days before winter," Amy said, "why don't we take a drive up north along the lake into the Green Bay area. We can hit all the cheese factories along the way."

"I don't know about hitting all the cheese factories, but I like your idea. The Rolls needs to be on the open road. It's been cooped up in the garage for too long. How about next week-end?"

They were barely into Wisconsin when Derek pulled the car over and stopped. Amy asked why they were stopping.

"To take pictures," he said.

"Right. That whole field of sunflowers. They are beautiful."

"And that house over there." Amy followed his hand and saw it. There was a house with a flat roof with grass growing on it and a goat feeding on the grass. He told her to open the glove box and retrieve the notebook and pen and write down the day and time of the picture of the goat. Derek felt one of the reasons his books were successful was because he allowed the reader to connect with the stories. Whenever and wherever he traveled he recorded unusual scenes like a goat eating grass on the roof of a house. He would incorporate that in a future story and a reader in Wisconsin would recognize that and feel a connection. They passed many cheese factories but only stopped at one. It was small and seemed to be family owned. Nevertheless, their selection of cheeses was more than adequate. The couple spent Saturday night in the Upper Peninsula and did a tour by boat of Green Bay, an arm of Lake Michigan.

Monday morning Amy knocked on Anna's cubicle and entered with two cups of coffee, one of which she handed to her colleague and told her she had news.

"You're pregnant," Anna said.

"No," Amy replied. "I went away for the weekend." Anna waited for the follow up. "With a guy."

"Great," Anna said, "you met a guy and were hiding him from me?"

"I met him about six months ago."

"Wait a minute. Are you talking about the guy you refused to date? The guy who was on welfare and a drug pusher? That guy?"

"I was totally wrong about him. He is not on welfare, not a drug pusher. He has a good job with a literary agency and makes good money."

"So, what happened while you were away. Did you...?"

"No, but we kissed a lot. I mean deep, curl your toes kisses."

"So, what are you guys waiting for? You need to take lessons?"

"I don't know. It just didn't seem the right time."

"Okay. I'm giving you two weeks and if it doesn't happen, I'm bringing my husband over and we'll show you how."

"You would too, wouldn't you?" Amy said.

"Damn straight."

A few days later Amy received a phone call to tell her the owners of her condo decided they no longer wanted to be landlords. They were putting the condo on the market. This was distressing news to Amy. She liked her condo on the lakefront. She could sit on her balcony and watch all the action in the park and on the lake beyond. Also, she enjoyed having Derek close by. It is possible the new owners would want to live in the condo. She told Derek of this new problem and he dismissed it with an announcement that he would lend her the money to buy the condo if she needed it. But she had to move fast before someone else grabbed it. She knew the asking price and she could come up with fifteen percent of it. Derek told her he would lend her the balance, but she refused his offer. It would not be good for their relationship, she said.

"What if I get laid off," she said, "and can't pay you?"

"Then I would send some people to break your knees," he said with a broad smile.

"It's not a joke, Derek," she said, "I don't own that job. I would much rather deal with a bank. If I can't pay they would only sue me or take the condo. My knees wouldn't be involved."

"Thank God for that. I like your knees."

"I don't know if a bank would lend me the money."

"Okay. I understand your point of view. I can help in this way. I will take you to my bank to talk to the manager. He is a personal friend. I will assure him you are a trustworthy person of high moral character, a person who honors commitments and also is a good kisser. I think I can persuade him to lend you the money. Make an offer on the condo before someone else does. We'll worry about the money later. I don't want you to move away. It will mean I have to move with you and that will be a nuisance."

"Really? You'd move with me?"

"Make the offer."

Amy had good relations with the elderly couple and when they found out she wanted to buy the condo, they dropped their asking price and she accepted. The next step was for Derek to take her to his bank to meet the manager whom she recognized, immediately, as one of his poker buddies. He remembered that one time when she brought in a basket of sandwiches for them. The process went smoothly and in less than a month Amy had become a condominium owner.

Derek didn't have to but he went with her to the closing and afterwards she took him to lunch to thank him for his help.

"You don't have to worry about your knees," he told her.

"No," she said, "thanks to you."

"I have a confession," Derek said.

"Oh, what?"

"The manager likes your knees too. He told me that when you brought in the sandwiches."

CHAPTER EIGHT

November came to Chicago by way of a cold wind blasting off the lake. At the beginning of the second week, Derek left for California to work on the movie, taking Amy with him. If November foretold what winter would be like they just might linger in California. But they couldn't because Amy had a job to return to. But it was nice to think about it. Amy had never experienced the making of a movie so it thrilled her to be there. She was even more thrilled to see how Derek was given VIP treatment by the studio and some of that rubbed off on her. After two weeks they boarded a plane to return home where her job and Derek's current project waited. Thanksgiving was coming up and she invited Derek and some of his single friends to dinner. Anna and her husband and two other ladies from her office were also invited. She was planning a huge spread and when Derek offered to help her she told him she wanted to do it alone. But when he insisted she gave him the job of carving the turkey and slicing the ham. Derek was not to be outmaneuvered, however. The Saturday before Thanksgiving a delivery man arrived with two boxes. In them were six bottles of wine and an assortment of liquor including Scotch, Bourbon, Vodka, Rum and Cognac.

"I received the care packages," she said after he let her into his apartment. "Thanks. Everything will go well with turkey and ham. How is the book coming?"

"It's not," he said, "my muse has departed. I think the cold has driven her away."

"You better get her back and soon. Your readers await the next best seller."

"So does my agent and my publisher is also making noises. Some of the action takes place in Peru, in Lima to be exact. I have been to Lima but it was some years ago, so I need to go back and refresh my mind. Can you get some time off to go with me? I know it is coming soon after you had your vacation, but it would only be one day. I can do everything in a long weekend."

"You want me to take a Monday off?"

"Or a Friday. Whichever would not put you in a bad light with your employers."

"It would help if I can tell them I would be traveling with D.R. Fisher."

"Maybe, but I'm not ready for that big reveal yet."

"Do your friends know your secret?"

"No. They only know what I told them, that a rich family member left me a large inheritance and I am currently managing it. Nobody has ever questioned me further. So, that secret is yours now too." She dragged a finger across her lips to seal them and pantomimed throwing away the key.

Amy was in for a big surprise on Thanksgiving Day. Every invited guest helped with whatever needed to be done. Obviously, they had been coached by Derek who acted like a foreman on a construction site. And Amy remarked on it. To which Derek replied, "if I'm the foreman of this motley crowd, you're the top dog, the big honcho, the owner." The dinner was one big, loud gathering of friends. Amy could not contain her joy at how things turned out. She had come to believe the day she met Derek was the day her life had been transformed. And to think she had rebuffed his invitation for coffee.

The weather turned brutally cold after the Thanksgiving holiday. The windy city was making every effort to live up to what some people named it. By now the original Algonquin name was lost to history and people simply referred to it as windy, because of the fierce winds that came off the lake and rattled people's bones.

Derek rang Amy's bell and when she answered she saw him standing there all dressed up.

"Out job hunting?" she asked.

"No, and I've got a problem," he said.

"Don't tell me. One of your readers returned a book."

"Has anybody ever told you that associating with me is bad for you? You've developed my fondness for sarcasm."

"Sit. I'll make us drinks then you can bare your soul." She disappeared into the kitchen and came back with two glasses with bourbon over ice.

"That's good," he said after clinking glasses and taking a sip. "My publisher wants to put my picture on my next book."

"I always wondered about that," Amy said. "This is bad, how?"

"The whole world will know who I am."

"And you're thinking that your readers will drop off if they know you're black."

"That was originally why I kept my picture off my books, but I don't think it matters anymore. Actually, my publisher thinks it might even increase readership."

"So, what's the problem?"

"I like my anonymity. I've grown used to it and I like it."

"Is the publisher insisting?"

"Not yet, but they will. Once they've become convinced that my picture will bring in sales, God Himself wouldn't be able to stop them."

"They probably have a point. A hunk of any color is still a hunk."

"I'm sure they didn't teach you that in accounting classes. So, you think I should pose naked for my picture?"

"If you did that your publisher wouldn't be able to keep up with the demand."

"So, you think I should go ahead and do the naked picture."

"Of course not. I don't want you being every woman's wet dream."

"I'll think on it," he said.

Two days later, Derek was returning from a shopping expedition when he realized there was movement in Amy's apartment. He put his bags down and listened at the door. There was movement in her apartment and it was too early for her to be home. He hesitated about what to do. He could call the police but he was not sure it was not Amy who had come home early. He rang her doorbell and was pleasantly surprised when she answered, but he could tell from her body language something was not right.

"What's wrong, Amy?" he said, "and don't tell me nothing. I can see you've been crying."

She told him that someone, a man, had called her office and informed the receptionist that Amelia Knight was consorting with a black man. Yes, he had used the word, 'consorting.' The receptionist mentioned the call to Amy's boss because it sounded ominous. The boss called Amy into his office and asked her if there was any truth to what the man said.

"And what did you say?" asked Derek.

"I told my boss I was indeed seeing a black man and was proud of it. And that I loved the man."

"And what did he say?"

"Nothing. He thanked me for stopping by although it was he who called me in. I'm sure it was Joseph Martini who made that call."

"Who is Joseph Martini?"

"The man whose jaw you broke."

"I thought he was in prison?"

"He threw himself on the mercy of the court and received a light sentence. He's probably out on parole. He can't come near me or it's back to prison, so he figured he'll get at me this way."

"Now, your entire office will know about your black lover. What do you think will happen?"

"Nothing. Nobody gives a damn. I am just upset my boss even discussed it with me. That's why I came home early. Would you like to stay for dinner?"

"Sure. I have groceries out by the door. Let me put them away. Be right back. I have some news for you, that might cheer you up."

The news Derek had for Amy, which he thought might cheer her up, would take her life in a new direction. His agent had expanded the agency beyond books and was now involved with actors. This meant he needed an assistant, preferably someone with a financial background. Derek had convinced him that instead of hiring an assistant he should take on a partner. The agent liked the idea but had no one in mind who could fit in. Derek told him he knew someone who might be interested. And by the way, this person is an accountant with deep financial experience.

Derek returned to Amy's apartment for dinner and sat at the kitchen counter while she busied herself getting dinner ready. He told her about his talk with his agent. She stopped in the middle of taking dinner out of the oven.

"You told him what?" she asked.

"I didn't promise anything. I told him I would talk to you." Amy burst out laughing.

"Derek, you know I'm in hock to the bank for this apartment. I don't have money to put into a partnership."

"I know that," he replied, "but I do."

"Derek, I'm not borrowing money from you to put into a partnership," Amy said, "let's not talk anymore about it

"I have to lend you the money," Derek said, "it's a black thing. You wouldn't understand."

"A black thing, huh. I wouldn't understand, huh. Don't you pull that race card on me."

"Funny thing about a race card. It works both ways. It can be for bad and it can be for good. This time it's for good." Amy burst out laughing.

"Well, I'll be damned," she said, "you're determined to continue turning my life upside down aren't you?"

"Somebody, I don't know who, said that was the definition of love."

CHAPTER NINE

Amy was not joking when she accused Derek of turning her life upside down. In the space of three months, she had gone from being an accountant to an agent representing authors and movie stars. She had also morphed into being a homeowner and a businesswoman. She was congratulating herself on the strides forward she had made until a phone call brought everything down around her ears. The call was from her mother. The same mother she had not spoken to in four months because they had been estranged for the past ten years. Her mother called to ask Amy why she was bringing shame down on the family. How could she allow herself to be seen in the company of a black man.

"Who told you that, Mother?" Amy asked.

"It doesn't matter who told me," her mother said, "is it true?"

"Considering we have hardly said ten words to each other since you left Daddy and ran off with another man, I don't see where it is any of your business."

"It is my business when you bring down the good name of this family. I am the laughingstock of the club."

"And you should be for what you did to Daddy." Amy was getting annoyed.

"If your father were alive he would be completely saddened by your actions."

"No, Mother, he was already saddened when you took up with your lover."

"You haven't answered my question," her mother said.

"I have not because it is none of your business. You forfeited your right to question me a long time ago. Goodbye." She disconnected from the call and slammed her fist on the kitchen counter rattling the coffee cup she was drinking from. She knew the person who called her was Joseph Martini. The sneaky coward. Her doorbell rang. It was Derek. She pulled him into the apartment taking him by surprise.

"Wow," he said, "that anxious to see me, huh. I stopped by to see if you want to go see a movie, but with such an enthusiastic welcome maybe we should stay home and do something else. If you get my drift."

"My mother called and wanted to know if it is true I am involved with a black man. This is the same mother who dumped my dad, and took off with another man. She didn't think that was such a shameful act. But my seeing you has those dried up biddies at her club all in titers."

"What does your father think?"

"My father passed away last year. I think he died from the shame of what my mother did."

"So, what did you tell her?"

"That it was none of her goddamned business."

"How did she find out?"

"I'm sure it was Joseph who made that call."

"I have a story to tell you." he said.

Derek's story took Amy back to when he was a boy growing up in South Side where, to survive meant being a member of a gang. He was never a gang member but he knew many kids who were. He was never pressured to join because, he was bigger and smarter than most of them. Plus, his father and his mother would have disowned him. So, he grew up surrounded by gangs but was never a part of any. His parents' one goal in life was to see he got a good education and leave South Side. He did that but retained his contacts in the neighborhood and he knew they were people there he could call on to take care of things for him. Amy was left staring at him at the implication of what he was saying.

"You mean…"

"I mean if this Joseph continues to be a thorn in your side, I could call on some people who could change his mind. They won't hurt him but they would scare the hell out of him with the promise if he did not change his ways, things could go badly for him."

"No, Derek," Amy said, "I could not condone violence."

"There won't be any violence. Only the promise of violence. You would be surprised what a great motivator that could be. Don't forget I make my living writing about this stuff."

"We haven't talked about our family backgrounds. Maybe this would be a good time," Derek said.

Derek told her about the love between his parents. He was an only child and his parents lavished all their love on him and made sure they gave him a solid foundation to start his life. They were so deeply in love with one another that when his mom succumbed to pancreatic cancer, his dad followed soon after.

"I think he died of a broken heart. He found living without her unbearable. So, I am really an orphan. I have cousins spread around but I am not close to any of them." He stopped talking and was looking at Amy with questions in his eyes. Her background was almost the opposite. She too was an only child but only because there was very little love between her parents. Amy always felt she was an accident. Her mother made her feel she was a mistake. Her family was one with resources and her mother flaunted it. Amy went to the best schools, they belonged to clubs and her mother was the social climber personified. She never got along with her mother and tried to free herself from any relationship with her. When her mother cheated on her father and left the family, it was the last straw. Her father died shortly after that and it was not from a broken heart. It was probably from shame.

"I've lost interest in a movie," Derek said. Amy disappeared into the kitchen and returned with two plates with apple pie on them.

"I've tried my hand at apple pie, and you better like it."

"Yes, ma'am. It looks really appetizing." Amy brought out one of the bottles of single-malt scotch, Derek had gifted her, with two glasses and a bucket of ice. They toasted each other and very soon Amy found herself slurring her words slightly.

"I should go," Derek said.

"No. Why?"

"Because if I don't go, things might happen"

"Things? What things?"

"This," Derek said and pulled her to him. Their lips found each other and Derek's hand wandered over her body causing her to groan with delight.

"I think you should spend the night," Amy whispered in his ear as she was nibbling on it.

"Yes, I should," he agreed as he started to unbutton her blouse. He then slid his hand under her bra and she groaned in response.

CHAPTER TEN

I t was January in Chicago. The holidays had come and gone and all the residents who were still in the windy city had hunkered down to survive the winter as best they could. Derek was standing on his balcony looking out over the lake. All he could see was ice extending to the horizon. There was a freighter in the distance trying to make headway against the surface ice and throwing chunks of it into the air. He called Amy and told her to come out to her balcony. He wanted her to see this. She waved to him when she came out. He pointed to the lake.

"What do you see?" he asked.

"Ice," she replied, "and there is a ship trying to best it."

"Does it give you any ideas?"

"Yes, that I should go back inside where it's warm."

That was not the idea Derek had in mind. They had no plans for the evening other than Amy had some contracts to look over and Derek was planning another chapter in his current novel.

But things can change. He rang her doorbell. He could have used the key she had given him but he preferred not to surprise her by walking in unannounced.

She opened the door and said to him, "we're not buying anything today," trying to look serious as she said it.

"You'll want to buy what I'm selling," Derek said, walking into the apartment.

"And what are you selling?"

"This," he said handing her a brochure that showed a beach with white sand and palm trees swaying in a gentle breeze.

"Flip it over" he said. She did and the next page was the same beach with moonlight slanting over the water.

"I see," she said, "you're selling sand, palm trees, ocean water and moonlight. And where would I be able to find all of these?"

"On an island in the Caribbean known as Barbados. All you have to do is pack a bag and I'll do the rest. You know how to pack, don't you?"

"And what do I tell my partner who would have to take over the appointments I have coming up?"

Derek had thought of everything. He would simply tell Amy's partner he had to do research for the book, in Barbados and he needed someone with Amy's talent to accompany him. After all, she was supposed to be his editor on this book. It was important she gain firsthand knowledge of the workings of the Bajan criminal mind. Amy was staring at him as he explained all this to her.

"Who are these Bajans?"

"That's what Barbadians call themselves. Let's run it up and see what happens."

"I can tell you right now. It won't fly. My partner did not get where he is by being a dummy"

"He is not. He also knows the importance of keeping his authors satisfied."

"So, you're planning to blackmail him. No pun intended."

"If I have to, yes."

It was barely two weeks later that Derek and Amy were going through security at Chicago O'Hare International Airport, on their way to sunny Barbados. To make it even more pleasurable, it had snowed the night before and Chicago was a cold, shivering mess.

They were sitting in the first row of the first class cabin. As soon as they sat down a cabin attendant approached and asked if they wanted something to drink .

"It would be another twenty minutes or so before we close the door," she said.

"I would," Amy said, "do you have champagne?"

"We do. And you, Sir?"

Derek looked out the window and observed, "it's snowing again. In a few hours we will be in the tropics. I'm starting my tropical experience right now. Can you make a rum punch?"

"Of course," the attendant said with a broad smile. "We have a whole batch already made. Good choice."

Amy held up her hand, "make mine a rum punch also." In a very short while the attendant returned with two glasses of rum punch.

"Made with Bajan rum," she said.

"I would like to ask you something, but I don't want to be rude," Derek said.

The attendant smiled and said, "I know what your question is and yes, I am Bajan."

Amy was staring at her as she moved off. "She's white," she whispered to Derek.

"Yeah, I noticed that too," Derek said and laughed. Amy knew he was laughing at her expense and she elbowed him. He offered her an explanation. Barbados was, at one time, a British Crown Colony and when it became a self-governing independent nation, many of the Brits who used to work for the British government, stayed on and took out Barbadian citizenship.

"That's why she has a British accent," Amy said. "I think I'm going to like this place. I might even consider becoming a Bajan."

Derek stared at her and was trying to think of something to say, but she put her seat back and closed her eyes. Derek dozed too and came awake when the attendant brought them lunch. He nudged Amy who also woke up to find lunch sitting on the table in front of her. The attendant asked if they would like another rum punch and they both said yes. Then she asked them where they were staying in Barbados.

"The Ocean Manor Resort," Derek said. "Do you know it?"

"Indeed, I do. It's one of the best on the island. It's on the Caribbean side which is the better. The Atlantic side tends to be stormy with high waves. Not very pleasant for swimming."

Now they were over open water and will be until they touched down at Grantley Adams International in Barbados. As soon as they stepped outside the airconditioned building they knew they had left Chicago far behind and were now in the tropics. The limo from the resort was waiting for them with another couple already seated in it.

"Definitely not Chicago," the other woman said, and they all agreed. To get to the resort they had to go through Bridgetown, the capital, which was a bustling tropical city of more than one hundred thousand people. And judging from the clogged streets they all seemed to be out and about.

Derek had arranged for a rental car to be delivered to the resort for them to tour the island. Their first stop was the area known as the North Point. It was the northernmost point of the island where the Caribbean Sea and the Atlantic proper, met. Th,e land was elevated creating a cliff that was at the mercy of high winds and battering seas. As the waves hit the cliff they sent sprays high into the air. Derek wanted to take a picture of Amy with a spray at her back. As he was centering her in his viewfinder a big wave crashed into the cliff sending, not just spray, but a volume of water over the cliff. The water hit Amy squarely in her back and knocked her to the ground and as the water receded it was pulling her towards the cliff face. Derek saw, with horror, what was happening, dropped his camera and raced towards her. He hurled himself through the air and pinned her to the ground, but that was not enough. The rushing water was so strong it was pulling both of them. A group of people who were also sightseeing saw what was happening and raced to help them. They grabbed Derek and Amy by their arms and was pulling when someone shouted, "hurry, another one is coming." They just barely got Amy and Derek to a safe place when another, bigger and higher wave hit sending even more water over onto the land.

Derek and Amy were sitting with their backs to a tree a safe distance away trying to absorb what had just happened.

"I almost died," Amy whispered, a sob lodging in her throat.

"*We* almost died," Derek replied putting his arms around her and holding her tight. He looked around to find the people who had saved them but they had already driven off.

"Derek," Amy said, "can we go back to the hotel. I'm not in the mood for anymore sightseeing today."

"I agree," he said and took her by the hand and headed to their car.

That night, at dinner, the manager of the resort introduced herself and told them she had heard of their misfortune at the North Point.

"I have never encountered waves that high at the North Point," she said. "We are all grateful to those people who just happened to be there. The mayor has ordered a metal barrier to be placed away from the edge of the cliff to keep people at a safe distance. Your dinner tonight is compliments of the Ocean Manor Resort."

She offered her hand to Derek who rose to shake it, and she waved to Amy. The rest of their sightseeing was more benign, the best part being their time in the sunshine. Reluctantly they were soon on their way back to the airport and on a plane to Chicago.

CHAPTER ELEVEN

It took Derek two more months to finish his novel. After it was proofread, he sent it to the agency and that is when Amy saw it for the first time. He refused to let her see it while he was writing it. He wanted her to see the finished product and not a work in progress. Derek had included their tropical adventure and when she read about Barbados it brought back pleasant memories. It also brought back the horror of their near death experience. One of the characters in the novel did die in much the same way they would have, if those strangers were not there to rescue them.

Derek's new novel was a success. This was the first book that sported his picture on the cover and it looked as if his publisher had made a wise decision to let his readers see the man they enjoyed reading. He was a little concerned his readers might be put off that he was black. The feedback from some people was that the reason D.R. Fisher wrote so compellingly about crime was probably because the author, himself, had done time. But such comments were few. The reviews were all positive and the reviewers declared D.R. Fisher had, once again, knocked one out of the park. Not only were sales skyrocketing but people who had not read his earlier books decided to go back and read them. So, sales picked up in those books also, and much to everyone's delight Hollywood came calling. A movie studio was interested in the book and was putting out feelers to the agency to explore purchasing the rights to it. Amy found out about this before Derek and was bursting to tell him the good news. This called for a special celebration and she was beaming when she rang his doorbell. She was practically jumping for joy when he let her into his apartment.

"Don't tell me." he said, "you won the lottery."

"Close," she said, "you're the winner."

"I don't remember buying a ticket."

"No, but you wrote a book."

She told him he had hit the jackpot in the form of a movie contract. Two studios were interested in making a movie of his book. The studio that made his earlier movies were offering more money for this book than they did for the other two because they were sure this was going to be an even bigger blockbuster. Then there was a smaller studio with limited resources who thought this movie could move them up in the ranks. She handed Derek two typewritten pages.

"I did some digging to find out about this smaller studio and this is what I came up with. Read it." She handed him her report. Derek scanned through the pages and laid them on the table.

"It's a no-brainer," he said, "the larger studio is offering me a much larger payday. Why not go with them? Am I missing something?"

"Do you have something I can highlight with?" she asked. Derek went to his office and came back with a yellow pen with a broad felt tip and handed it to her. She went through her report stopping to highlight certain lines and passages. She handed the report back to him with the advice he should pay particular attention to the highlighted areas. He read it again this time taking his time and her advice. When he was finished he put it on the table in front of her. She had highlighted, BLACK FEMALE DIRECTOR, TWO BLACK FEMALES ON BOARD OF DIRECTORS, DIVERSE CREWS MADE UP OF PEOPLE OF DIFFERENT ETHNIC BACKGROUNDS.

"Correct me if I'm wrong," he said to her, "aren't you the same woman who said to me, and I quote, 'I don't date black men?'"

"True," she replied, "but haven't you noticed how I have grown?" He looked her up and down, noticing her shining blond hair to her shoulders, her tall, athletic figure that belied her age, her legs that went on forever.

"I see the same beautiful woman I have always seen," he said.

"All the changes are on the inside. Not physical."

"Ah, yes," he admitted.

"Derek, have you noticed the more you associate with me, the wiser you become?"

"That's something my dad would have said. You haven't been communicating with the dead, have you?"

"Nooo. That would scare the hell out of me."

In the end Derek decided to take a chance on the smaller studio who clearly saw this as a chance to vault into the big leagues. Further research had shown they had the talent if not the money. But with a contract in hand, they were able to get financial backing. After Derek's decision to go with the smaller the studio, Amy asked him how he felt about going out on a limb to help the little guy get a leg up.

"Good," he replied, "I have not forgotten, other people went out on a limb for me."

CHAPTER TWELVE

Spring had come late to Chicago that year, simply because winter was reluctant to release its grip on the city. On the first warm day Derek invited Amy to go for a ride with him. When she asked where they were going he said it was a secret. As they progressed south Amy realized they were heading into South Side, and became alarmed. Derek noticed her unease and reached out to take her hand.

"Have you ever been in this part of Chicago?" he asked. She shook her head, no.

"Okay, a quick lesson. South Side is made up of several areas ranging from the very affluent to the very poor, from practically no crime to crime ridden. I come from an area that is very multi-cultural and multi-ethnic. That's where we're headed." He got off the main thoroughfare and turned down a street that was lined with middle class homes that were well kept up. He stopped in front of a single-family house with a small garden in the front. There were pots of flowers on the steps leading to the front door.

"That's where I lived," he said, "I don't know the family who owns it now. I had already moved out when my dad died, so I just sold it. A real estate company bought it from me and resold it." As he was telling this to Amy a very large black man rapped on the driver's window. Amy immediately went into defense mode. When Derek had reconditioned the car he had installed electric windows and doors. He pushed the button to roll his window down and a huge smile broke out on his face. He reached out and grabbed a huge paw.

"I'll be damned," Derek said, "Joseph Johnson. Amy, this is a friend from my youth. Everyone calls him JJ. This is Amy Knight." He punched a button to unlock the rear doors. "Get in," he said.

"I live just across the street," Johnson said, "come in. We'll catch up. When I saw the car I knew it was you because you're the only ni... you're the only person of color who drives a car like this. It turned out to be one fine ride. You did a great job."

As soon as they entered the neat house Johnson went into the kitchen and brought back three beers. "Sorry Amy," he said, "I should have asked if you drink beer."

"I do. Thank you."

"So, JJ, how is the old neighborhood?'

"Improved the day you hauled your ass out of here." JJ replied.

"And what are you up to?"

"I don't know where to begin. After you left and I didn't have to spend time protecting your ass, I studied and got my GED. Then I attended community college and got my associates degree. Now, I'm a manager at Southie's Markets."

"They're still around, huh."

"Bigger than ever. Tell me, how did you end up with such a fine-looking woman? She blind?" This brought laughter.

"Luck I guess," Derek answered, "and no she's not blind. What about you? Found a woman who could tolerate you?"

"You remember Louise Masters? As I recall you had a thing for her. Well, she finally agreed to be my wife. We have a boy and another kid in the oven."

"You wore her down, huh."

"Didn't have to. I just used my charm and sweet personality. Enough about me. I want to hear about you and your beautiful companion here."

The two friends talked for about two hours and JJ, much to Derek's surprise because the big man was not how he remembered him, took pains to include Amy whenever he could. On the way home, Amy said, "I like JJ, I would like to meet his wife. Especially since she's the woman you had a thing for."

"What JJ didn't tell you is, I was twelve years old at the time."

"Does he know you are a best-selling author?"

"Probably not. He would have made some reference to it. He will find out soon enough. As I recall that supermarket where he works has a book aisle. The book with my picture will find its way there eventually." It did not take long.

JJ called and after congratulating Derek on his book, told him the entire community is brimming with pride. It happened JJ was straightening the books on the shelves when he picked up a book and there was Derek staring back at him. He always knew his old buddy was destined for greatness but this was beyond anything anybody dreamed. D.R. Fisher was his boyhood friend, Derek. If that didn't beat all. Word spread quickly and very soon they were organizing a 'local boy made good' party in his honor. They were inviting every important person in Chicago and of course everyone from the community would be there. There were very few success stories from the South Side. This one was going to be shouted to the world. Derek told Amy about it and her first words were, "I have to go shopping for a new dress."

"Is that all it means to you?" he asked.

"You want me to look good, don't you?"

"You would look good in a flour sack," Derek said, "but I expected a more prideful response."

"Come over here and I will show you how prideful I am." She opened her arms and he walked into them. Then he bent down and found her lips. Then he picked her up and carried her into the bedroom. And then there was no need for more talk.

CHAPTER THIRTEEN

Derek was standing at Amy's door when she answered the bell, with his hand behind his back.

"What are you holding behind your back?" she asked him.

"This," he said and presented her with a rose.

"Oh my," she said, "a single red rose. Thank you. Do you know what this means?"

"That I'm too cheap to buy a dozen?"

"No. It means love eternal. Forever."

"I was hoping you'd say that," he said, bringing her hand to his lips.

"We have an important anniversary coming up," Derek continued..

"What anniversary?"

"It was one year today when you said, and I quote, 'I don't date black men.'"

"Are you ever going to let me forget that?"

"Sure, in another fifty years."

"I would prefer to celebrate our first kiss. And yes, I would prefer to forget that statement."

"Okay. Since you've made all my dreams come true, we can forget you said what you said."

"Thank you and since you've made all my dreams come true I'll treat you to dinner tonight. You can name the restaurant."

"You may regret saying that," Derek said with a smile.

"We'll see," Amy said, returning his smile.

The restaurant that Derek chose was on the Navy Pier, just a few blocks from their condo building. Parking in that area was known to be difficult so they took a taxi instead of Derek's car.

The restaurant was known for its barbecue and the great view it offered of the lake. Derek ordered cocktails after they were seated and while they waited for the drinks he told Amy about an idea that came to him..

He was thinking of buying a condo in a warm place where they can escape to when the Chicago winter became too much to handle.

"You're probably thinking of Florida," she said.

"Yes, and not only Florida but the Florida Keys."

"Aren't they a little too rustic for a city boy like you?"

"No. The rusticer, the better."

"Rusticer? Did you just make that up?"

"Probably, but I'm a wordsmith so I'm allowed." Their drinks came before they got deeper into Derek's claim to reinvent the language. The server approached with her pad to take their dinner orders. They had not looked at the menu but Derek looked at Amy and said, "ribs?" She nodded yes.

"Barbecue ribs," he said to the server, "with everything that comes with it."

After the server left Amy said, "tell me more about this idea of yours, of escaping to the Florida Keys, during winter. Remember, I don't have the luxury of working from home as you do."

"True, but since you are a partner and not just an employee, you can probably work out a deal whereby you spend less time in the office. I am not talking about spending the entire winter in Florida. There are things we enjoy here in the winter. I am talking about a couple of weeks here and there. And if you get any problems from your partner, you can always take your money out and open your own agency."

"What? My own agency? Are you serious? Do you realize I would have to work harder than I do now."

"I know that, but you would be able to regulate when you work at the office and when you work at home without the inconvenience of a partner being upset with you. I think a lot of what you do could be done from a home office. I'm just thinking out loud. Give it some thought. Just so you know, there are at least six established authors, including yours truly, who would come with you."

"So, you're saying while my employees are freezing their butts in Chicago, I could be warming mine in the Keys."

"In a word, yes," Derek said, just as the server brought two heaping plates of barbecued ribs with all the accompaniments. They stopped talking and fell to the business of eating. Halfway through Amy put down her fork and regarded Derek. "Your idea has merit," she said, "there is a 'but.' I don't like the idea of stealing clients from my partner."

"Yes, I see your point. You'll just have to work at getting new clients. As I said it is just something that occurred to me." They let the topic drop and moved on to something else.

Three days later, Derek was helping Amy clear dishes from the dinner they just had in her apartment, when she asked him, "how are things coming with your condo in Florida?"

Derek let out a hearty laugh and answered, "about the same as you opening your own agency."

"In other words, nothing."

"In that exact word."

Amy asked him if he had any idea which Key he was thinking of. He had not thought that far yet. He had spent time in the Florida Keys doing research for an earlier book, so he knew the Keys. They all appealed to him including Largo, Matecumbe, Islamorada, Marathon and of course, Key West. If he bought property it would be a condominium because of the convenience of maintenance. Then something happened to put a hold on his plans. Amy's partner announced his retirement and asked her if she were interested in buying him out. When she told him she did not have the funds to do that, he proposed they make a contract for her to pay him over time. He hinted that such an arrangement might suit him better because he liked the idea of getting a paycheck every month or every quarter whichever they decided.

CHAPTER FOURTEEN

"Well, that makes our earlier discussion, moot," Derek said, when Amy told him. "How do you feel about that?"

Amy didn't know how she felt about it. She and Derek had talked, hypothetically, about her having her own agency, but now that she was faced with the reality that it might happen, she was a little ambivalent. She found herself focusing on the negatives. Things like did she have the experience to take on such an endeavor. Or what if she crashed and burned taking other people down with her. Derek knew it would take all his persuasiveness to convince Amy to take the leap.

The conversation flowed back and forth examining all sides of the problem until Derek threw in something that gave Amy pause.

"Your partner is determined to retire," Derek said. "He will sell his interest to someone. What if that person is not a good fit with you?"

"Not fair," she said. "You've just introduced something that scares me."

"But a reality, nonetheless," Derek replied. Nothing more was said until one afternoon Derek was in his office working on his new project when Amy used her key to enter his apartment.

"Say hello to your new agent," she said, beaming.

"You did it," he said throwing his arms around her. "Congratulations."

"I did. And just you know, your new agent is going to be a lot tougher. No more missing deadlines or moaning how you need time off because it's too cold."

Derek was looking around her.

"What are you looking for?" she asked.

"Your whip."

Derek was not at home when Amy arrived from her office, but she soon heard him on the catwalk. He was passing her door when it flew open and Amy grabbed him and pulled him into her apartment. She pulled him to her and kissed him until he was fighting for breath.

"My God, woman," he said, "what got into you? You took my breath away, literally."

"I need a favor," she said.

"If it has anything to do with that kiss, I'm in." Amy went into her office and brought out a file which she handed to him.

"These are three chapters of a manuscript that came to us. It is written by a female author who is a person of color. I would like you to read it and give me your opinion."

"How do you know she is a person of color?"

"She said so in her biography." Derek tucked the file under his arm and continued to his apartment.

The next evening, he was at the mailbox when Amy entered the building and went to her mailbox. They rode up together.

"Did you read that manuscript?" she asked.

"I did. Let's get into your apartment and we'll discuss it." Amy brought out a bottle of wine and two glasses and they settled on her sofa.

"So?"

"So. I know agents are always on the lookout for that gem that would turn into a best seller." Amy said nothing, waiting for Derek to wind his way to the finish.

"Since you asked for my opinion I assume you want me to be honest. I think what you've found here is trash."

"Oh? Explain, please."

"These pages are nothing but one sex scene after another. If there is a story here, I didn't find it. It seems the main characters are obsessed with sex for the sake of sex, with each other and with other partners. This book has nothing to offer a reader unless that reader is looking for pornography. You'll never sell this manuscript to your usual publishers and if you send it to any of them it will damage your reputation. You'll have to look in the pornographic aisle. It may sound as if I'm stereotyping the author but I'm not. There are many great authors of color. This is not one of them." Amy was smiling as he was talking.

"Why are you smiling? You've already decided to turn it down."

"I have. I wanted to get your opinion You're right about the stereotyping thing. You're not. Most of the manuscripts we get are from white people male and female and a many of them are garbage. Occasionally we come upon a gem and gems come in all colors."

"And so does trash," Derek added. Amy told him she was putting on her agent's hat and asked about his current book. He told her it was coming and she told him that was not good enough.

"Do you browbeat your other authors like you do me?" Derek asked.

"No," she replied, "but they are not my lover who lives next door."

A week later Derek asked Amy if she could take a long weekend off. She told him she couldn't that weekend but, maybe the next. Why what plans did he have?

"Nothing yet," he said, "but I would like to go down to the Florida Keys to look at condos."

"That's still in play?" she asked. It was in play. Derek had it all planned and two weeks later, on a Friday, they were in Chicago O'Hare on their way. They flew into Miami, rented a car and drove down to Homestead where they spent the night. Next day they continued on, arriving in Largo at mid-morning. Derek had made appointments to see condos all along the Keys as they headed to Key West. They saw nothing they liked until Key West. They found a three bedroom apartment on Roosevelt Avenue about a quarter mile down from the airport, overlooking Smathers Beach and the ocean. It was exactly what

Derek had in mind for a winter getaway. Why three bedrooms Amy wanted to know and Derek explained. One bedroom for sleeping, one bedroom to be turned into office space for both of them, and one bedroom for a guest if anyone turns up. The condo building was new and there were just a few apartments left. Derek immediately made an offer for the one they were standing in. He was looking at the beach, the ocean and the pool off to the side. All the appliances were new and it came with space in a garage under the building. Derek declined the realtor's offer to put in an application at a bank.

"I have my own source of financing," he told the man, and then asked, "how soon can we close? Plan it for a Saturday"

The Saturday of the closing they spent only the one night and were back in Chicago late Sunday evening.

"How are we going to manage furnishing the condo?" Amy said.

"That realtor gave me the card of a designer in Key West. I'll contact them and put them to work furnishing the place, including our office with computers and whatever equipment we need."

"I would like to come in with you as a partner," Amy said.

"Thanks. But that's not necessary. You're still paying off your former partner in the agency. When you're done with that we'll talk again about a partnership with me for the condo. Fair enough?"

"Fair enough," she said.

CHAPTER FIFTEEN

It took Amy two years to do it but she finally made the last payment to her former partner. The agency was now totally and officially hers and she had grown it. Derek asked her a question that made her think for a couple of minutes. "Am I the only brown horse in your stable?" She stared at him not fully comprehending what he was asking, but burst out laughing when she got it.

"I don't know," she said, "I have not checked the pedigree of the other horses. You're the only one I ride all the time."

"We have an anniversary coming up," Derek said.

"Right. Our first kiss. Isn't it strange, most people celebrate their engagement, their wedding or other big events. We mark the anniversary of our first kiss."

"That's because it was a momentous occasion. When I pulled you in to kiss you, I wasn't sure you wouldn't slap me."

"I couldn't. I had fallen in love with you. How about you?"

"Ha. I fell in love with you the first time I laid eyes on you. I felt, given enough time. you would see I didn't belong in all those boxes you had put me into."

Derek and Amy lived on the fifteenth floor of their building and their balconies afforded a panoramic view of the lake and part of Chicago including the Chicago River. They were looking at a tour boat on the waterway and Derek said, "that's something we've never done. I read they have dinner tours on the river using larger boats. Let's mark the anniversary of our first kiss with a dinner cruise on the river." Amy agreed and Derek said he would make the arrangements.

"I have a question about that kiss," he said. Amy waited for it.

"I've been thinking it might be a good idea to include a little more romance in my novels and..."

"Your female readers will love you for it," Amy interrupted.

"I want to know how did it feel kissing a man of color for the first time? I know you had other boyfriends. Did it feel different?"

"Yes it did. Not because of color but because I truly love you. I didn't really love those other guys. I didn't see your color. How about you?"

"Well truthfully, I have not kissed a man of any color." She punched him in the gut.

"You know what I'm asking."

"My answer is the same as yours Color disappeared."

They walked from their building to the boat terminal and boarded a luxurious boat with the beautiful lines of a yacht. The dining area rivaled that of a five-star restaurant only smaller. They sat in the forward section and allowed themselves to be thrilled seeing their city from the water for the first time.

"This is the best way to celebrate our first kiss," Derek said. He looked around and saw that everyone on the boat was intent on watching Chicago slide by, so he took the opportunity to gather Amy in his arms and kiss her. He did not care if anyone saw him. Nor did Amy judging from the way she returned his kiss.

"Let's do this every year," she said, and added, "I mean the boat tour, not the kiss."

"I am glad you clarified that. I don't think I can wait a year to kiss you."

Summer was just starting and Derek and Amy were spending the end of winter in their condo in Florida. Amy was in the kitchen putting the finishing touches to breakfast and Derek was in the living room watching the news on television. He sat up straight when the weatherman announced a front he was monitoring, was on the verge of becoming the first hurricane of the season. The storm was named Abigail, Abby for short. Derek mentioned it to Amy at breakfast and she had questions. She wanted to know if they had already laid in a track. They had not. It was too early, but the weather people were carefully monitoring Abby's movements.

Their plans called for them to leave in a week but now they were not sure what they would do. They hoped that by the time of their departure the weather people would have a better idea of where Abby was headed. Three days later Abby was a category three hurricane churning her way across the Atlantic. Derek stayed glued to the television hoping to get an idea as to what he and Amy should do. Neither had been in a hurricane before so they had no sense of what that was like. They knew that safety had to come first, even if it meant leaving Key West early. There was no defense against a hurricane except getting out of the way.

They were due to leave on a Saturday morning and it was now Thursday. Abby had strengthened to a category four and had her eye set on the Bahamas chain of islands. Derek tried to change to a flight on Friday but all flights leaving Florida on all airlines were booked. Their only chance was the flight they were confirmed on for Saturday. The forecasters were now almost certain they knew where Abby was going. She had left the Bahamas and was making a beeline to the Miami area, but she had grown so large the outer bands of her winds extended five hundred miles out and that meant Key West would catch heavy wind and rain. Key West was low-lying like most the keys so the water was the bigger enemy. Then it was announced on television that all Saturday flights out of Miami were canceled. Amy and Derek were stuck in Key West to ride out their first hurricane. They followed the advice given on television as to what preparations they should make. Their condo was practically on the beach with nothing standing between them and the wind and water.

The officials had urged everyone to get into shelters if they thought they were vulnerable. Derek reasoned that since their building was built on columns extending ten feet into the air, their apartment was safe. Not so their rental car which was at ground level under the building. They made the decision to hunker down and ride it out in their apartment. The wind that was coming into Key West was considerably less powerful than in the Miami area. Their problem was the Atlantic Ocean that was at their doorstep.

By the time Abby reached the Florida coast, she had remained a category four but had shifted course slightly to come ashore north of Miami, in the Boca Raton area.

As Derek expected, the wind was not a problem, but he watched in dismay as wave after wave breached the seawall and rolled under his building demolishing all the cars parked there. It took four hours for the ocean to quiet down and the water to stop going over the wall. Derek ventured out and found all the cars piled up against columns. He couldn't even find his among the jumble. He heaved a sigh thinking about the paperwork the rental company would require to put in an insurance claim. When they had planned this trip they had considered driving down. Now he was glad they did not. It would have been heartbreaking for him to see his beloved Rolls smashed up against a column. The airline promised to call him as soon as flights returned to normal. In the meantime, he was able to rent another car from a company in Key West. He did not have to wait long for that call and on Sunday they were on their way back up the Overseas Highway to Miami and their flight home.

Derek was quiet on the drive and Amy mentioned it. "Just thinking," he said.

"I know what you're thinking," Amy said. "You're thinking that surviving a hurricane would make a good chapter in a novel."

"Yeah. Might be a good way to get rid of some bad guys," he answered.

CHAPTER SIXTEEN

Amy braced Derek about a topic she'd been avoiding but no longer could. "Have you thought about having children?" He put down his coffee cup and looked at her.

"Where is this coming from?" he asked.

"Just wondering. My biological clock is running down. For all I know it has probably already stopped. But your boys could still swim."

"My boys? Where did you hear that expression?"

"I read it in a book I'm thinking of representing."

"If you're thinking of fixing me up with another partner…"

"Hell no. If you want to feel the wrath of a scorned woman try going down that path."

"Okay. Your question. I'm an only child, no brothers nor sisters. I've never given any thought about having children. You?"

"Sometimes. But that thought doesn't stay with me long. I am not sure I want the complications children bring. As far as I am concerned the status is quo."

Amy rang Derek's bell and when he answered he asked her, "lost your key?"

"Just didn't feel like fumbling in my purse for it."

She had news for him. It appeared his record of being the only brown horse in her stable was about to be broken. A query came into the agency from a woman of Chippewa ancestry. In her letter she mentioned that Spring Flower, Derek's friend, had recommended she contact Amy's agency. She was a new writer and this was her first book but the blurb and the chapters she sent in showed a writer with promise. Yes, Derek remembered Spring Flower. He had lost touch with her, partly his fault. She had written to him when she went back to North Dakota but he had forgotten to reply. He will now. He pointed out to Amy he was still the only brown horse she could ride that is until she did a search, which she was not interested in doing. At any rate, he considered Indians the first people to inhabit this continent, and were, therefore, in a category all by themselves.

They were sitting on Amy's sofa having a glass of sherry when she unbuttoned her blouse and began feeling around her left breast. She had felt a soreness in it and wanted to make sure there were no lumps. She didn't find any but asked Derek to verify she was free of lumps.

"You want me to feel you up?" he said, his face covered with a smile.

"This is for health reasons," she said.

"Right," he said and started to do as she requested. It may have been for health reasons but she was enjoying it. "No lumps," he declared.

"Try the right one," she said with a whimper. He set to the task and soon his own sexual desire got the better of him and he bent down and took her nipple into his mouth. He heard her intake of breath and a weak "I didn't ask for that, but don't stop."

"Couldn't help myself," he said and started to undress her. They made love on her sofa for the first time. It was a little short for Derek's long frame, but they managed. Afterwards they lay wrapped in each other's arms and dozed. Amy went to see her gynecologist immediately and after an extensive examination she was pronounced free of any cancer she might have suspected. The doctor assured her that she might have strained herself during her gym workout. It turned out the soreness was not in her breast but in the area surrounding her breast.

Derek was having a difficult time with his current novel. He could not make it come together. He had planned thirty chapters like his other novels, and he was writing chapter sixteen but it was a struggle. By this point the words should be flowing and the novel should be writing itself but that was not happening. He asked Amy to read what he had written so far and give her opinion. He was hoping that another pair of eyes might spot something. Amy was reluctant. She reminded him that he never liked anyone to read his work until it was finished, but he convinced her to look at it.

It took her three days to read the chapters he had given her.

"Why so long?" he said.

"I read it three times," she said, "and I can tell you, this is not you. This is not D.R. Fisher. I get the feeling you're trying too hard to write the great American novel."

"Too many big words?" he asked smiling at her.

"The big words didn't bother me. I kept a dictionary handy. It does not flow the way your words usually flow."

"If it's flow you want I'll give you flow. I am scrapping what I've written and starting over. It is not the first time I've had to do that."

"Ataboy. You sound like D.R. Fisher right there." Derek was already leaving her apartment when she said, "where are you going?

"To write a novel. One that flows."

CHAPTER SEVENTEEN

Derek kept at it night and day. After he left Amy he spent the better part of the evening staring at his computer, willing the words to come but they did not, until the next day. He lay awake and after discarding all thoughts of the novel he had started writing, a new idea blossomed in his brain. He knew what he wanted to write and started and the words came and came. He did not stop for breakfast until he had exhausted the current supply of words. D.R. Fisher was back at work. By the time he stopped he was well on the way to creating a new novel, one that would hold up to the expectations of his readers.

That evening Amy walked into his apartment and found him in his office at his computer. She invited him over for dinner but he begged off. He said his brain was full of words that needed to be let out, so he could not stop. She buzzed his lips with a quick kiss and told him she would bring a sandwich over for him. He acknowledge it with a wave of his hand without even looking at her. He was on a mission to give his readers what they expected and more. Derek hunkered down in his office with a determination to finish this new novel by the original date. Amy gave him the space he needed and never complained.

One evening she arrived home from work to find him sitting in her apartment with a drink in his hand and a smile on his face.

"Since you're here lounging, I take it the job is done," she said.

"You take it correct. I'm sending it to your office by email tonight. It will there when you get into the office tomorrow."

"Can I read some of it now?"

"Nope. You have to wait for the full manuscript."

Amy went in early the next day to start reading Derek's new work. She read two chapters, turned away from her computer and stared into space. Her secretary found her in that state and asked if she was okay. She replied she'd never been more okay.

"We have a new novel by D.R. Fisher and if the first two chapters are any indication, we have another best seller on our hands."

'"You mean Derek, don't you?"

"Derek Roberts, D.R. Fisher makes no difference. This is gold. Read it for yourself."

"I'll print it up and take it home tonight."

Amy could not resist calling Derek to congratulate him.

"You've knocked it out of the park again," she said.

"I take it you like what you've read," he said, "but would the publisher?"

"I can sell this to any publisher out there. Don't be surprised if a movie deal comes along."

"I like an agent who is enthusiastic about her authors," Derek said.

"And I like authors who write best sellers," Amy returned. She spent the rest of the day getting deeper into the novel and the more she read the more convinced she became she had a best seller that would spend a long time on anybody's list. She decided also to play hardball with the publisher and ask for a larger advance. If they balked she will go to another publisher. She knew this novel was a moneymaker and they would know that too.

After Derek disconnected from Amy he was in a reflexive mood. He knew his parents would have been proud of him. They were the ones who pushed him to get an education convincing him that the only way to succeed is through education. He was happy with his life. He was in love with and loved by a beautiful woman who truly cared about him. Derek was a happy man until the day it all came crashing down.

CHAPTER EIGHTEEN

It was Saturday morning. After breakfast together Amy announced she needed to do some clothes shopping. She was going to take a taxi but Derek convinced her to take his car.

"You're offering me your car, your baby?" She was incredulous.

"Didn't we agree what's mine is yours and vice versa?" he said, "besides people will see a beautiful woman in a beautiful ride. Take the Rolls."

Amy was stopped at a red light when the driver's door flew open and strong hands grabbed her and yanked her out of the car, throwing her to the ground. She hit her head on the pavement and crumpled to the ground. The man who had pulled her out hit the button to unlock all the doors and two other men got in, one in the passenger seat and the other in the back. The light changed to green and they took off. The driver in the car behind hit his horn in an attempt to stop them, to no avail. He jumped out of his car and began to motion for other cars to move away from the body on the pavement and at the same time he dialed emergency. It was not long before an ambulance arrived along with two police cruisers.

The medics knew at once that Amy was in bad shape. She was unconscious from the blow to her head and bruised and bleeding. They bundled her into the ambulance and took off, sirens blaring. The man told the officers he had witnessed the whole thing and could give a description of the three men. He also told them the license tag caught his attention because it said WRITER. He told the police where to reach him if they needed more information.

The officers conferred among themselves and decided it was a carjacking. The man had said it was a Rolls Royce so they thought a car like that would end up in South America with a drug lord. Their priority was identifying the woman who was attacked. They thought, correctly, the thieves would most likely go through her purse, take what was in it and toss the purse out the window. They left their cruisers parked and started to walk in the direction the Rolls took. Two blocks later they came upon the abandoned purse. The money was all gone but all her cards were there including her driver's license. They now knew who she was. One cruiser took off for the hospital with the identity of the victim. Fortunately, she also carried a card with Derek's name as the person to call in an emergency. Derek was watching a ball game when the call came. He immediately turned off the television and hurried to the elevator. He hit the ground floor running and hailed the first taxi he saw.

Amy was surrounded by nurses and doctors when he arrived in the emergency room. She was just waking up and when she saw Derek she started to scream pointing at him. The doctors and nurses were at a loss to explain what was going on with her. One doctor took him outside to ask who he was. Derek showed him his license and explained he was a friend. The cop who had taken the other driver's statement was still there and related the conversation he had with the witness.

"You say three black men?" Derek asked.

"That's what he said," the cop replied.

The doctor locked eyes with Derek and they both nodded. Amy saw a black man enter the room and did not remember Derek. The doctors had said she'd suffered temporary amnesia. It would be best if Derek stayed away until she regained her memory. Derek agreed, but he had no intention of leaving the hospital. He would stay in the background until Amy was better. Later that evening they decided to test her. Her doctor asked a colleague, who was black, to accompany him to visit Amy. She was fully awake and as soon as she saw the black doctor, her eyes went wide. She did not scream but her eyes never left him. She was wary of him and watched his every move. Derek was waiting for them outside the door.

"Her memory has not fully returned," the doctor said, "she did not scream but she was wary. Her eyes never left Dr. James."

Derek was beyond angry. One way or another he was going to make these men pay. The police had told him their assessment of the crime as a carjacking to get a luxury automobile. It was quite possible it would be shipped out of the country. He kept checking on Amy and was elated when the doctor told him she had shown signs of complete memory recovery. Derek was going to test her. With the doctor by his side, he walked into her room. When she saw him her eyes lit up and tears were forming. She raised her arms, ignoring the bruises and the tubes, for him to hug her. He did gladly. The doctor patted him on his back and left them alone. Now that Amy was on the mend he turned his attention to the carjackers. He intended to bring these guys down.

He called JJ to ask how he should go about achieving what he wanted. After he gave his friend a detailed account of what happened, JJ told him to sit tight he would get back to him. He had an idea. True to his word, JJ called and told Derek to come to his house to discuss what could be done. When Derek arrived, there were six men in the living room. Introductions were made and Derek recognized two of the men from when he was a boy living in that neighborhood. All six of these men were big. They looked like the defensive line of the Chicago Bears. A couple of them had bulges in their pockets which indicated to Derek they were armed. And that bothered him. He wanted revenge but not death. He wanted his car back but it was not important.

They told Derek they had an idea where the car was headed. They were going to talk to some people and come up with a plan in a day or two. They will let JJ know and he will get in touch with Derek.

"JJ," Derek said, "I don't want anybody killed in this."

"No, no, bro' nobody is going to be killed. We don't want a murder trial in our neighborhood. The brothers are gonna ask them very polite, please give the car back. You say your lady got hurt, right? Well, there's gonna be a payment for that. By the way they're gonna have some expenses."

"I understand. I'll cover all expenses."

They kept Amy in the hospital a couple of days longer to make sure all her brain functions, including memory, had returned to normal. She had spent four days in the hospital by the time Derek picked her up in a taxi.

"I'm sorry about your car," she said.

"Don't worry about the car," Derek said, "it's insured. I'm just happy to have you back whole. As for the car the police is on top of that." He did not mention anything about JJ and his gang.

"I would suggest you take a day or two at home before you go back to work."

"No, I'm fine. I had a nice rest in the hospital. Now I'm ready for work."

Joseph Johnson called the next day. Derek was glad Amy had gone back to work. It avoided the necessity of a lie when he went out.

CHAPTER NINETEEN

JJ had told him to bring money but he didn't say how much. He said he didn't know how much the men would need so Derek went to his bank and withdrew ten thousand dollars and hoped that would be enough. Johnson was alone when Derek arrived.

"I told you to come a little early before the others got here, so we can talk," Johnson said. Derek nodded.

"They know who took your car and hurt your lady. Your car is in Miami and they know the location. It's waiting for a ship to take it to Venezuela. Three guys're gonna fly down there and grab it and drive it back. There are guys in Miami that will help them if they run into any trouble, but we don't expect any. Here they come. Be cool."

Each one of them high-fived Derek when they came in. Derek took Johnson's advice and stayed cool. He waited for them to talk.

Ironically, the smallest of the bunch appeared to be the leader. "We traced your car," he said, "the idiots left your plate on so it was easy to track down. We're not dealing with a lot of brainpower here. George, Dude and me are gonna fly down there and grab it and drive it back." Derek held up his hand to stop him.

"The police know about the carjacking," he said, "if you get stopped..." he left it open.

"You got a point, maybe you should come with us and drive it back yourself. Tell the police you located it yourself. Means they don't have to keep looking. They'd love that. We're gonna need some bread."

"How much?" Derek asked.

"We figure that with the airline, hotels, maybe something for the dudes in Miami and something for us here, we're looking at eight thousand dollars." Derek looked over at Johnson and he nodded.

"Okay." Derek said. "When?"

"Give the money to JJ. We'll figure a time and he'll call you. Couple days. The car's not going anywhere, no boat leaving for another couple weeks."

As Derek sat in a taxi homeward bound he was thinking how he can leave for maybe four days without telling Amy what was going on. There were two things Derek was sure of. One, he was dealing with a vigilante group and his good friend JJ, the supermarket manager, was the head of it. And two, he was going to lie to Amy. The question remained which was the smaller lie. He got it. He will tell Amy the police tracked down his car in Miami and he was going to fly down there to pick it up. The lie was the police did not find the car, vigilantes did. Then he came up against another problem. What if she wanted to go down with him?

"The police in Miami called," he told her. "They found my car. They suspect it was going to be shipped out of the country."

"That's great," she said, "when are you going?"

"As soon as I can make the arrangements. In a couple of days."

"Wish I can go with you, but I've got a lot on my plate right now."

"That's too bad," he said and was about to add he was hoping she could come, but decided to hold his tongue. No point in compounding the lie and having her say maybe she could make the time.

Two days later Derek was in Miami with three of the vigilantes. They were met by a man holding a bag which he handed to the one named Dude. They rented a car and drove to a warehouse on the outskirts of the city. Derek's Rolls was parked outside in view of everyone. It occurred to Derek that criminals all seem to operate with half a brain. They slowed and Derek pointed to his car.

"That's mine," he said.

"Nice ride," one of the men said. "I heard you rebuilt it yourself."

"Took me three years," Derek said.

"Okay, this is how we gonna do this. We gonna leave you at that café we just passed. JJ said we shouldn't involve you. You just the owner come down to drive your car back. We go get your car and bring it to you, then you take a nice drive back to Chicago. How we do this is not your business." Derek nodded and got out of the rental and went into the café.

The three men went into the shack at the back of the lot, and the man sitting at a desk by the door greeted them.

"Help you?" he asked.

"Yeah we want to buy one of them cars. I kinda like the Rolls Royce. How much you askin'?"

"These cars ain't for sale," the man said.

"You sure? How come they sitting out in the lot?" A door in a back room opened and a man stepped out.

"You heard what he said. Now beat it."

"Man, you sure unfriendly. I just asked about buying one of them cars and you come out and be nasty." Three guns suddenly jumped into hands of the visitors.

"You want to try and talk nice? I think I know what's going on here. You in the export business and them cars are heading outa the country. Why didn't you say so in the first place?"

The men in the office said nothing. They just kept their eyes on the guns. Dude walked to the rear and looked in the office. It was empty. So, this was a two-man operation. He came back to the front.

"Both of you step over here near this pipe," he said pointing his gun at the pipe that ran from the floor to the ceiling.

"What if we don't want to?"

"That will be a big mistake. This here gun has a tricky trigger it could go off accidental when I'm pointing it at you, like this," he raised the gun and aimed for the man's head.

"Hey, Dude," George said, "you don't have to kill him. Just aim for his knees."

"Why didn't I think of that?" Dude said pointing and firing. The sound was deafening in the enclosed space. He missed.

"Damn. I missed. I never miss. One more time." He prepared to fire but the man screamed.

"Stop. Stop. I'll do what you say."

Dude told him to produce the tag the car came with.

"It's in the back. Which car?"

"The Rolls. I'll come with you to make sure you find it. And I need tools."

The man came out with the correct tag and some tools which he handed to Dude who gave it to George. who left to attach the tag. Dude then motioned the two men to put their hands behind their backs. Sammy produced handcuffs which he used to chain the men to their own pipe. By then George came back in and placed the tools on the desk.

"Okay," Dude said, "we gonna say so long, amigos. We taking the Rolls and we gonna tell the police to come rescue you. 'Course you gonna have to explain to them how come you have all these cars in your lot waiting to be exported. I'm gonna tell them you in the export business."

Dude got in the Rolls and George and Sammy got in the rental and they drove to the café to meet up with Derek. When Derek saw his car approaching he came out and shook their hands. He got in the Rolls and started the long journey back to Chicago after retrieving his overnight bag from the rental. Dude, George and Sammy headed for the airport to return the rental and board a flight that will take them home. They high-fived each other for a job well done, and nobody got hurt. What the Miami police does with those two guys was none of their business. Just as they were leaving, a car drove up, and Dude handed the driver a bag and the two men bumped fists..

CHAPTER TWENTY

Derek had plenty of time to think about the men who had hurt Amy. He was glad to have his car back but he was not satisfied. He felt he needed justice for Amy. She could have died after being flung from the car. If a good Samaritan was not behind her she might have been run over by another car. Derek hurried home to see Amy and to show her he had his car back. He also wanted to see Joseph Johnson to ask his help in resolving the unfinished business with the three hoodlums.

Derek rang Johnson's doorbell and a woman with two children came out. Derek recognized her.

"Louise," he said, hugging her, "as pretty as ever."

"Derek," she said, "still have a silver tongue."

"Well, look at you. Married, two children."

"And one in the oven," JJ hollered from inside the house, "honey don' spend too much money."

"He'll never change," Louise said shaking her head.

Johnson invited Derek in and brought out two beers one of which he handed to Derek. He told Derek that since his phone call he and his 'boys' had given some thought about what needed to be done.

"We know there is a debt to be paid to you and your lady. To your lady mostly. Me, I am a respectable manager of a grocery chain with a beautiful wife and children, but some of the boys don't have, shall we say, my sense of respectability."

"JJ what I said earlier still holds. I don't want any killings."

"No, man. We're not going to kill anybody. We don't operate that way. Now, if the police found out about the chop shop those three operate and they raided the joint and somebody got hurt, well that's not our problem. And you and your lady will not be involved."

"You know where such a place is?"

"Oh yeah. But you don't know and don't need to know. It will cost you some more bread to put it into operation. Just keep your eyes on the newspapers." Derek agreed. He could not imagine how they would get the police involved without bringing Amy into it, but he trusted JJ.

Another carjacking occurred on the streets of Chicago. This time the driver who was pushed out onto the street was run over by a passing car and died on the way to the hospital. This time it was murder. JJ's people had positive proof the same three men were involved .

A call came into the Police Station from a concerned citizen who identified the jackers and the location of their operation. The concerned citizen hung up before he could be questioned further, but he did say the police had to act quickly because the car would be spirited out of the city very soon. The police acted. That same afternoon a contingent of unmarked cars bearing officers in riot gear surrounded the shop. The three hoods had no idea cops were on their trail until one of them happened to walk outside and saw the unmarked cars. He suspected immediately it was the police because those cars were not there an hour before. He rushed back inside and alerted his gang that the police was on to them. They consulted among themselves that the best course of action for them was to get into one of the cars and make a run for it. Big mistake.

The police were out of their cars and hiding behind open doors when a high powered car blasted out of the garage, turned on two wheels and headed down the street. The police opened fire peppering the car with bullet holes. More than one bullet pierced the wind shield and struck the driver in the face. He died instantly causing the car to wrap itself around a tree. The man in the passenger seat also died but the one in the back seat saved himself by ducking down behind the front seat. He was still alive when the medics arrived, but with broken limbs. They hauled him off to the emergency room for treatment. It turned out his injuries were even more severe than first thought. There was damage to his spine and the diagnosis from the doctors was that he probably would not walk again. In addition to that, the police was going to charge him with accessory to the murder of the driver whose car they had carjacked and who died as a result of it.

Amy was reading the newspaper when she came upon the news of the carjacking and its aftermath. They had printed pictures of the jackers.

"Those are the same men who attacked me," she said, "according to the news they were the ringleaders of a carjacking outfit."

Derek read the news account and felt justice had been served. The only role he had played was to put up the money for it to happen. And his friend Joseph was not even involved. Of course, Derek had no idea who the concerned citizen was who started the ball rolling.

As for Amy, she said she never liked people to be killed, but she could not feel any sympathy for those men who almost killed her.

Derek felt a chapter had been closed satisfactorily.

CHAPTER TWENTY-ONE

Exactly as Amy had predicted, Derek's new novel went straight to the top of the charts. Amy received a call and noticed on her screen her mother was calling. For a brief moment she considered not answering, but she knew her mother would keep it up until she connected. She answered and after a stilted greeting her mother stated why she was calling.

"I would like to come for a visit," the elder woman said.

"Why?" was Amy's terse response.

"I would like to end this estrangement between us," Angelina Knight said. "It is not natural a mother and daughter should be so distant from each other. I would like to be a part of your life."

"Mother, let me say this upfront," Amy said, "if you're coming here with the intention of driving a wedge between Derek and me, save your time and money. Don't come."

"No, no. that's not why I'm coming. I really would like to begin a relationship with my daughter. Let's call it mending some fences."

"You do remember it was you who put holes in those fences."

"Yes and now I would like to mend them. Well, I would like to remove them altogether so that nothing stands between us."

They talked for a long time with Angelina saying she would make arrangements and call back when her plans were made.

"My mother is coming to visit," Amy told Derek

"Should I make myself scarce?" he asked.

"No. We live our lives as we always do. She'll have to fit in or don't bother coming. I told her as much."

Three days later Angelina Knight was at Amelia's door.

"Mother," Amy said, "I could have picked you up."

"I didn't want to bother you, and I know you don't have a car, at least you didn't the last time we spoke. A taxi was fine."

"Well come in. Make yourself comfortable."

"There is one thing I would like to get out of the way and then no more will be said. I would like to meet your Derek. I think I should know the man my daughter is in love with."

"Okay, I'll take you to him."

"Is it safe? Why don't you have him come here?" Amy assured her mother it is quite safe to visit Derek. And no, she did not need her coat.

"It's a little chilly outside. I think I brought some Wisconsin weather with me."

"We're going just next door, Mom"

"He lives in this building?"

"He does. Long before I moved in."

Amy used her key to enter Derek's apartment and her mother's eyes bulged when she saw that. This is very serious, she thought. Amy yelled out for Derek when she entered.

He came out of his office telling her, "I ain't deaf. You don't have to shout. Oh, excuse me." He noticed the older woman.

"Mom, this is Derek Roberts. Derek, my mother Angelina Knight."

Derek put out his hand. "A pleasure to meet you Mrs. Knight."

Angelina did not take his hand because she was too busy staring up at him. He was much taller than she was so she had to bend her neck. Her gaze was fixed on his face

"Mom," Amy said, "you're staring. That's rude."

Angelina ignored her daughter. "Do you know you're the spitting image of D.R. Fisher?"

"The writer?" Derek asked.

"How do you know that, Mom," Amy asked.

"Amelia, I am the president of our book club and D.R. Fisher is an author we discuss a lot. At our next meeting we're going to talk about his latest book, which, by the way, is a best seller."

"Have you read it, Mrs. Knight?" Derek said.

"I was the first one to buy it. And yes, I've read it and I think it's the best thing he's done. I don't know how he'll be able to top this book."

"So, you like Fisher's books," Amy said.

"All that I've read." Derek told them he was going into the kitchen to make drinks and he came out with three glasses with rum punch. Angelina took a sip and declared it was very refreshing. Amy and Derek exchanged eye contact and he gave her permission.

"Mom, the reason Derek is the spitting image of D.R. Fisher is they are one and the same."

"What? What do you mean?"

"D.R. Fisher is the pseudonym I write under," Derek said.

"You mean..."

"Yes. You've just met your favorite author," Amy said.

"Oh my God," Angelina sputtered, "oh my God. Wait 'til I tell the ladies at my book club I shook hands with D.R. Fisher. They'll faint."

"Well, that is not exactly true," Derek said, "we haven't actually shaken hands yet."

"Right." She stuck out her hand, "Very pleased to meet you Mr. er, do I call you Mr. Fisher or Mr. Roberts.?"

Derek took her hand. "Derek will do. It's the name my mama gave me." Amy touched Derek's shoulder and beckoned him into the kitchen.

"Mom, will you excuse us for a minute?"

In the kitchen Amy said, "You've just made a convert. If you would like to make a friend, offer to come to her club and talk to the ladies."

"You've made an excellent point. I'm all for making friends."

They returned to the living room. "Mrs. Knight I would love to come to your club and chat with your ladies."

"Oh my God. I better sit down."

"Mom you're already sitting."

"Oh, but Mr. er, Derek, we couldn't afford you. I'm sure you demand a lot of money for an appearance."

"How about I come at no charge? But you have to promise to let the ladies know that I am coming to see them because you're a friend of mine."

"Don't worry. They'll know that and also you're my daughter's man. I only hope none of them have heart attacks when they learn what a great thing I've done."

The conversation continued allowing Angelina to re-establish a relationship with her daughter and to get to know her daughter's lover. Angelina thought for a while and then said, "I would like to take you two to dinner. I hear there are some fine restaurants here in Chicago."

"Yes. We do have a couple of good restaurants here in the city," Amy said and smiled at Derek. "Derek will make a reservation."

"Good. I'll pick you up in a taxi," Angelina said.

"That won't be necessary, Mom," Amy said, "Derek has a car. We'll pick you up at your hotel." Wait until she sees a Rolls Royce pull up to the front door of the hotel. One more reason to brag to her book club.

Angelina gazed at the luxurious car that cruised to a stop in front of her. The doorman opened a rear door and handed Angelina into the luxurious interior of the Rolls Royce Silver Cloud.

Derek was driving, with Amy sitting next to him in the passenger seat.

"I feel like a queen," Angelina said, "I can't believe this car. I've ridden in luxury cars before but nothing like this".

"I'll tell you a little secret," Amy said, "this car was totally run down when Derek bought it. He refurbished it himself."

"Took me three years," Derek said.

Angelina spoke barely above a whisper, "I've missed so much, haven't I?"

"True," Amy said, "but that only means we have lot of catching up to do."

They were seated in the restaurant when Angelina broached the subject of Derek's visit to her book club. How does she go about it, she wanted to know.

"Don't worry, Angelina," Derek said, "Amy is my agent. She knows my schedule and she will work out date and time with you. Talk with your ladies and men about it and then contact Amy."

"We meet in a small room at the library. When word of your coming spreads, they will have to give us a larger room. We have a membership of twenty-five but only about ten meet on a regular basis. When they hear you're coming, everybody will be there and the library staff will want in, not to mention other library patrons."

"Sounds like you have your work cut out for you," Amy said.

"I do, but I'm going to love it."

CHAPTER TWENTY-TWO

Angelina had convinced her favorite bookstore to sponsor the event. They billed it as a Meet and Greet best-selling author D.R. Fisher. Amy flew up to Green Bay with Derek the day before and while Derek stayed out of view at the hotel, Amy and her mother went to the library where the event was scheduled to take place, to check out the venue and make sure everything was in place. The library had assigned the largest room they had which looked like a small auditorium. There were piles of Derek's book off to one side and a table with a microphone. A bookstore employee was delegated to walk around with a hand-held mic which would allow the audience to ask questions during the question and answer period.

The day of the event the manager of the bookstore introduced himself to a packed room and after saying a few words about the author, turned the microphone over to Derek with a "ladies and gentlemen I give you D.R. Fisher." Derek came out of the shadows and bowed to the audience, thanking them for coming out. He thanked the bookstore for sponsoring the event and the library for donating the space. He also gave a shout out to Angelina's book club for getting the whole thing started. Then he talked about his book. He looked around the room and said, "I'm assuming you all bought copies. If you haven't there is a pile over there where you can get a copy and check to see if I lied about anything." This brought laughter. He warmed to his subject and spoke at length about what went through his mind while he was writing. He opened the floor to questions and a lady raised her hand prompting the worker to take the microphone over to her.

"What I want to know is this. Are you married? Your bio doesn't mention that." Several hands went up. "Me too." "I want to know too." It seemed as if all the women wanted to know Derek's marital status including a young man sitting in a corner with his hand up. Derek pointed at him.

"You have a question?"

"Yeah. I'm asking for my mom. She's divorced and too shy to ask for herself." The room tittered.

"Are you gonna answer?" someone shouted.

"No, I'm not married but I'm keeping company with a beautiful woman who is the girl of my dreams."

"What's her name?" came from the back. The worker realized they didn't need the microphone so she stayed where she was. "I want to know too."

"I am not telling," Derek said, "but I may give hints in a future book so you'll just have to keep buying my books if you want a name."

"What does D.R. Stand for?" another question shouted out.

"Nothing right now but I may give some hints in a future book, so again, you're just going to have to invest in another book."

"I gotta tell you," a man said, "you sure know how to sell books. I run a promotion company. If the book business dries up, come see me." There was laughter all around.

Derek brought the session to an end by telling his audience that he would be happy to autograph any book brought to him, even an earlier one if anybody brought one.

The line of people with books in their hands stretched out the door. The pile was visibly lower. All in all, it was a good day for the book business. The man who had offered him a job approached with his book.

"My job offer still stands," he said, "but from the looks of it, the book business is still solid."

"I'm impressed," Amy said.

"I am too," answered Derek, "the manager of the bookstore was pleased with the number of books they sold."

"I'm not talking about books," Amy said. "I'm impressed with the number of women who want to marry you."

"What you're saying is that I'm a viable commodity not only as an author but as a hunk."

"Hunk? Who said anything about hunk?"

"What do you say we close down here and head back to the hotel, so I can show you what I mean by hunk."

CHAPTER TWENTY-THREE

When word got out about the success of the event in the library in Green Bay, other bookstores were clamoring for D.R. Fisher to visit them. Derek had already started another project but he had to set it aside to go on tour. He welcomed this interruption because he was not totally committed to the story he was writing. Once again he thought his muse had deserted him so he would go on tour, sell books and interact with his readers. He would have liked Amy to accompany him but she had to beg off. The best she could do was to meet him at one city along the way.

She chose Atlanta. She would fly to Atlanta, spend one night with him and return to Chicago the next day. Derek would have liked more time with her but he knew she needed to be in her office and accepted Atlanta, telling her he would take whatever time she could give him.

"Just don't accept any marriage proposals," she chided him. It was in Atlanta that Derek came face to face with his harshest critics. And it had nothing to do with his book.

The largest bookstore in Atlanta had scheduled the book signing for 11:00 am, and the plan was for Amy to spend the night before with him at his hotel and accompany him the next day to the bookstore. Everything went according to plan until 10:30 am on the day of the event. They had an early breakfast in the restaurant in the hotel and returned to the room so Derek could get his notes. The telephone in the room rang and Derek answered it to find the manager of the bookstore on the other end. The manager told him to turn on the television to the local news station and call him back. A frown crossed Derek's face and Amy saw it as she was coming out of the bathroom.

"What's going on?" she asked, "why are you frowning?"

"I don't know yet. The manager of the bookstore called to tell me to turn on the television. He said they are showing something I should see. He sounded upset."

Derek turned on the television and the station was showing a woman standing on the sidewalk in front of the bookstore with a sign held over her head. The sign read, FISHER STICK TO YOUR RACE. The woman was black. Derek had no comment but Amy could see a rage building in him.

"Oh my God," she said, "how could she know? We haven't publicized our relationship."

"It doesn't matter how she knows. We have not been exactly secretive, but that is beside the point. It is nobody's business who I date. I will not stand for it." Derek called the manager back and told him that nothing's changed. They will be arriving at the bookstore as planned. He took Amy's hand in his.

"I'm sorry," he said, "if you don't feel comfortable being at the bookstore, you don't have to come. I will understand."

"You're not going without me," Amy said. "That woman with her sign is of no consequence to me. I don't care who knows or approves of us. I am not going into hiding. I should probably stand next to her with a sign that reads MIND YOUR OWN DAMN BUSINESS."

"If that's the way you feel let's go sell some books."

By the time their taxi pulled up to the entrance of the store, another woman had joined with a similar sign. She was white and a news reporter was interviewing them. When the reporter saw Derek and Amy he hurried over with his microphone out.

"Mr. Fisher," he said, "can I get a comment from you about this?" He waved at the two women with their signs.

"Sure," Derek said and paused for a moment looking at the women, "I am glad to see the races uniting in a common cause." This was not the comment the reporter was expecting so he tried Amy. She looked the women up and down and answered, "I totally agree."

Derek and Amy moved forward, entered the building and found the room where the event was being held. The manager welcomed them and introduced the best-selling author. Derek thanked him and the people who had come out to meet him. But before he began to speak on the main topic that brought him and them out, he knew he had to address what was going on outside on the sidewalk.

"Before we get into my book," he said, "I want to say a few words about the scene on the sidewalk."

"What did you tell them?" someone wanted to know.

"I told them I was glad to see the races united for a common cause." This brought some laughter. "I will not allow anyone to make dating choices for me.. Now let's get on to the business that brought me here from Chicago. My book." The manager had left the room while Derek was talking and came back to whisper in his ear. Derek nodded.

"I've just been told the two ladies have left. If this happens again in another city my response will be the same." The discussion that followed his talk was the liveliest so far on the tour, and Derek was pleased that no one seemed interested in talking about his choice of personal relationship. The line of people wanting him to autograph their books was long. The manager was all smiles and complimented himself for bringing in the author. He sold out his inventory and immediately placed a call to the publisher for more.

Both Derek and Amy were also pleased. They had come to Atlanta to sell books and did. They were having lunch when Derek's face broke into a broad smile.

"Can you stay another day?" he asked, "this is my first time in Atlanta and I would like to look around a bit."

"Mine too," Amy said, "let me make a phone call to move an appointment."

"Great. I hear Atlanta has a very vibrant jazz community. Almost as vibrant as Chicago. We can visit a club or two."

CHAPTER TWENTY-FOUR

Derek arrived back in Chicago exactly one month after he'd left. Amy was at the airport to meet him and they fell into each other's arms. In that month he had visited six cities, talked to many of his readers, which he thoroughly enjoyed and sold more books than he expected. The bookstores were glad, his publisher was glad, he was glad and even Amy benefitted financially from the tour. He was exhausted from the constant running to catch flights, getting on and off airplanes and trying to doze in seats that were not built for his length, even in first class. He was due for some down time and he decided he would take a couple of days off and do nothing. The project he had started could wait another two or three days. His cell beeped and when he looked at the screen it was his old friend Joseph Johnson. He had not spoken to JJ since that fiasco with his car. After greeting each other Joseph told him he had heard about his set-to in Atlanta.

"I have a brother in Atlanta and he knows we know each other. He said he saw it on the news."

"Yeah," Derek said, "it was a surprise."

"My brother told me what you said to that woman. It was priceless. I would like to see you, man. Have a lot to tell you."

"I'm coming into the city on business," JJ added, "let's do lunch."

"Do lunch?" Derek asked, "when did you start talking like that?"

"Ever since they made me general manager for our territory. We've expanded quite a lot and now I'm in charge of five stores. I'll tell you all about it when we meet."

Johnson was dressed in a business suit when he met Derek at a downtown restaurant. "I almost don't recognize you," Derek said.

"Yeah. You like the threads? It goes with my new position."

Johnson's company had bought out a string of smaller groceries in and around Chicago and had leaped into the big leagues, opening an opportunity for him to become a part of the management team. After they were seated, Derek asked him about his family.

"They're all good," he said, "three kids now."

"Any in the oven?" Derek asked.

Johnson burst out laughing. "Nope. Oven's closed for good."

"You mean you and Louise don't..."

"No. no. She decided three kids are enough. Had her tubes tied."

"How do you feel about that?"

"It's her body. She has a right to do what she wants with it. Besides, I agree. Three kids are enough." They kept the conversation going catching up with each other's lives. Johnson mentioned that with his new position came increased responsibility but also increased income, so he was thinking of moving out of the old neighborhood.

"Nothing's wrong with the neighborhood, mind you," he said. "You and I grew up there and look how we turned out. But, let's face it, the temptation to go over to the other side is always there. Louise and I want to remove our kids from that temptation."

"Are you thinking of leaving Chicago?"

"Oh, no. We love Chicago. We just want to be in a better part of it. We've wanted that ever since we got married and now I can afford it." They spoke so long lunch spilled over into the dinner hour

"I think they're giving us the evil eye," Derek said. "They want to set up for dinner." Derek signaled for the waiter and the check. When it came Johnson grabbed it, telling Derek lunch was on him. He considered it a business lunch and it was covered as expense. When they parted the two men hugged and Johnson told Derek he should come for a last look at the neighborhood before he moved away and he should bring Amy with him.

Derek received a letter from the Dean of language studies at Northwestern University in Evanston. The Dean was asking him to stop by, at his convenience, to discuss Derek joining the faculty to teach a course on the Novel. Derek was ambivalent because, although he could write a novel he was not sure he could teach one.

"They're not opposed to each other," Amy pointed out.

"True," Derek answered, "but they're not equal either. I write at my own pace, except when my agent is flogging me. Teaching a course means preparing lectures, reading and grading papers and all those things that tie you down. What's more it will cut into my writing time and that is my first love."

"You sound like a man who has decided not to take a job."

"No decision yet. Just thinking out loud."

Derek called the Dean's office and told the secretary to let her boss know he would stop by. He asked the secretary what would be a good time for his visit. She told him and they agreed on the time. As soon as he arrived the secretary immediately showed him into the Dean's office and the two men shook hands. To Derek's surprise the Dean was not what he expected. This man was almost as tall as he was and solidly built. He looked as if he could have been a member of the University's football squad.

"I'm guessing you played for the team," Derek said.

"All four years I was here. Got in on a football scholarship. Spent two years in the NFL until an injury put paid to my career. I hired on here as a coach and took courses for my PhD. One thing led to another and now I'm Dean of the language school. Don't ask how I went from football to languages; I probably could not explain it except while I was playing football I was interested in languages. You couldn't tell by looking at me but I speak three of them. How about coffee and I think Jean, that's my secretary, brought in some buns."

"Thanks. That would be good."

The Dean got out of his chair and went to the door which he opened and asked Jean to bring two cups of coffee with cream and sugar and two buns if they were any left. Shortly after, Jean appeared with a tray with the coffee and fixings and two buns.. The men talked football while they consumed the coffee and buns. Derek had played in college but was never good enough to make the 'A' string. The interest was not there. He was more interested in reading and writing and, he added with a smile, girls.

"So how do you feel about joining our faculty?" the Dean asked.

"It's quite an honor," Derek said, "but I'm going to pass. Judging from the reception my books get I can assume I'm a good writer, but I know I would be a lousy teacher."

"You're also an honest man who knows his capabilities and his limitations. I understand teaching a course might cut into your time as a writer and having read your books I wouldn't want that. Would you be willing to drop by occasionally to talk, informally, to those students who show promise as writers? We have a writers club on campus headed up by a faculty member. She would jump for joy if I told her D.R. Fisher would be stopping by."

"I can do that," Derek said. "It would be no different than the groups I talk to now. Tell her to call my agent to set it up. She knows my schedule." He reached into his pocket, took out a card with Amy's name and number and passed it over.

"Do you have an idea what the cost would be? Universities are always broke."

"Oh, I forgot to mention, there wouldn't be a charge. Someone told me it's called giving back to the community."

Later, that evening, Derek told Amy about his visit with the Dean. And if the Dean's secretary calls and asks Derek to come to the campus to talk to some students, could she please make him available.

"And I suppose it will be pro bono." Amy said. He put his arms around her and drew her in for a kiss.

"You're not only a fantastic agent, you're also a mind reader."

"I can read only one mind. Yours."

"And yours too, of course."

"Mine?" she asked, "ha. Most of the time I don't know what day of the week it is. Since we are on the subject of books, you have a deadline coming up."

"I was not aware we are on the subject of books."

"We are now. You know what are the consequences of missing."

"I know. You'll want your pound of flesh."

"No, but you will owe me a night on the town."

"You're a hard woman Amelia Knight." He still had his arms around her and she did the same to him. He kissed her again, this time with intensity. They were standing in her dining room with her back to the dining table. He very slowly eased her down to the table and got busy with his hands. She did the same with her hands.

"There is no telling the different uses one can put a table to," Derek was able to get out.

"For a best-selling author, you talk too much. Show don't tell."

Derek stopped the telling and got busy with the showing much to Amy's delight.

CHAPTER TWENTY-FIVE

Seventy per cent of the authors Amy represented were male and she wanted to change this ratio, so she actively sought out female authors. She launched a campaign on social media encouraging female authors to send in their manuscripts and many did. She hoped for an increase in submissions but was not ready for the onslaught which swamped her. All her readers were choked with work and Amy now wondered if the idea to solicit manuscripts was a good one. One thing she was sure of, she had built her agency's reputation to be of the highest quality and she would not jeopardize that by offering less than quality manuscripts to publishers. When the agency was owned by her former partner, he had ventured into representing actors, but when Amy took over she had allowed that part of the business to slide. Not only was it difficult to do this at arm's length from Hollywood, she also really had no interest in it. Authors were her only interest especially since the star of her stable lived next door and she was in love with him.

Derek was sitting in her living room when she arrived home from the office. She always felt special whenever he surprised her by being in her apartment with a drink at the ready. Her face lit up when he embraced her. He took her briefcase from her, set it down on the desk in her home office and placed a drink in her hand. They clinked glasses and each took a first sip.

"You certainly know how to welcome a hard-working lady," she said.

"Of course," Derek replied, "you trained me well."

They eased down to the sofa and Amy kicked off her shoes. Derek lifted her feet and put them on the coffee table, then he took off his shoes and placed his feet next to hers on the table.

"Tell me about your day," he said. "Judging from the weight of your case I would say you brought home a lot of work."

"Can't help it. We're swamped. I'm beginning to question the advisability of launching that campaign to get more female authors. I think every female who can punch the keys of a computer is writing a book and sending it to me."

"Are you getting quality books? Books you can sell?"

"I think the ratio of fantastic to good to horrible is the same as for my male authors. That's no surprise. I just never expected to be swamped. The problem with my business is in order to find the gleaming nugget I have to sift through a lot of dull, boring, not well written slush. And that takes time and energy. My assistants are at their peak now."

"I can help," Derek said, and Amy looked at him, wondering. "I can help by ordering in dinner right now."

"Oh. Yes. Thanks." She tried to keep disappointment out of her voice but it must have seeped through and Derek caught it.

"I can also help in another way," he said, choosing his words. "I can set aside some time to read for you."

Amy stood up immediately and shook her head, "no, Derek. I can't ask you to do that. You need time to write."

"I was keeping this as a surprise. What if I tell you I'm just about ready to submit. Another day or two should do it."

"Do you really mean that? And you will read for me?"

"I do and yes."

"What would I pay you. I'm your agent. I sell your books. This will be a first in the history of publishing."

"My fee is ten kisses per book.

"Ten kisses? I'm prepared to pay twelve."

"Then twelve it is. One kiss to seal the deal." She was still standing so he pulled her down and found her lips.

After dinner he helped her clear things away and led her to her office. "I'm going to leave you to your reading. Don't stay up too late. Remember what they say about Rome."

The next evening Amy handed Derek a paper bag with six manuscripts with a "thank you. And remember what they say about Rome."

Derek sent his own manuscript off to Amy and settled down to read what she had left with him. The first one he picked up was a book of poems. While he enjoyed reading poems, he was sure Amy's agency did not handle poetry. He turned to her published description of what the agency did not represent and poetry was one of the genres. This writer had completely ignored the requirements or did not bother to read them. While he might have liked to read the poems, there was no time. He took out a sheet of paper and wrote 'we do not handle poems' on it and stuck it in the manuscript. The next was science fiction, another 'we do not handle' book. Obviously an author who did not read what the agency was asking for. The third manuscript however was different. From the first line Derek was intrigued. He liked how the author had accomplished getting him interested. He was beginning to think Amy had another best seller on her hands, but as he read further he began to recognize words, phrases and sentence structure. Then it hit him with a hammer. He was reading one of his earlier books. The author had lifted whole sentences and paragraphs from one of his books. The only writing that was the author's own were the names of characters, and even here he came close to copying.

Derek put down the manuscript and thought long and hard what he should do. In his bio the author had said this was his first book. Derek had no interest in pursuing this in a court of law and possibly ruining the writer but he had to stop what he started doing. He decided to discuss it with Amy and she in turn with his publisher. He read no further and set the manuscript aside. He went to his personal library and pulled out the book he knew was plagiarized and began a comparison. He found, to his horror, many paragraphs were copied word for word. He circled them and referred them back to his book, so Amy could see.

Derek remembered, as a new writer, he was deep into a story when he realized he was writing words that had sprung into his mind. They sounded familiar and he was shocked when he discovered he was writing the words of one of his favorite authors. He did not mean to plagiarize the man's work, but he had done it subconsciously although not to the same extent. He had taken the only avenue left to him. He scrapped the project and erased it completely from his computer's memory.

Amy was astounded when she saw that. The author had a generic name that could be either male or female, and the bio made no reference to the sex. Not that it mattered. Plagiarism by either sex was still plagiarism and had to be stopped.

"How do you want to proceed?" she asked Derek.

"I don't want to go after any financial damages. I would like you to send a strongly worded letter, pointing out the exact words, phrases etc., that were plagiarized and to let the writer know what he or she has done was not only illegal but immoral. Hopefully that would be the end of it. You have to make it clear this is an infringement on another author's copyrighted work and your agency will not tolerate it."

"It is said imitation is a form of flattery. Do you feel flattered?"

"Hell, no." Derek was surprised she said that, "I work my butt off to make sure my words mean something and that the reader is invested in my stories. No, I'm not flattered. I view this person as a thief."

"Now that we've settled how we will proceed," Amy said, "would you like an advance on your one book twelve kisses contract?"

"Oh, I would like that. I will never turn down a chance to kiss you. How many do you have in mind?"

"Let' s start with one and see where it leads," she said opening her arms to him.

CHAPTER TWENTY-SIX

For the next month Derek concentrated on reading manuscripts from other writers and Amy declared he had been a great help to her. She even joked that it would take a lifetime to pay the debt she owed him. He told her he didn't mind how long it took; he was just happy to receive payment every time she paid. He then told her he would like to run an idea he had for another novel, by her. It was not fully developed yet, but a parallel theme was a fictional city in which the population was mostly interracial and therefore most of the children would be biracial. It would not be the main theme but a part of it. Amy waited for more but when there was no more from Derek she asked him, "are you going into science fiction?"

"No," he replied, "I like what I write. This would be a special place which would exist somewhere in our world. I guess what I'm asking is do you think you could sell it."

"Derek," Amy said, "you're a talented writer. I'm sure you could do justice to a story like that but I don't think the publishers who put out your books would buy into a book like that. Publishers are used to having sales as their goal and they wouldn't see sales in a book with that theme. Also, your readers have come to depend on you telling a story they could lose themselves in. I am not sure they would like such a story. You may lose readers."

"Okay, I get what you're saying," Derek said. "I don't want to go down the path Herman Melville did."

"Melville was a great writer. *Moby Dick* is the standard most novels are measured by."

"True. Now. But there is a backstory to *Moby Dick,* that I came across when I read about Melville. As a young writer he wrote books that people adored. He was the darling of the Saturday Evening Women's Club because he wrote books they could picture themselves in. For a week or two they could forget their troubles and pretend they were the beautiful young ladies being courted by the dashing lovers. He wrote books they could lose themselves in. But he was not satisfied. He wanted to write the Great American Novel so, he wrote *Moby Dick.* It was not well received. The critics thought this new novel will force readers to think and that is not what they wanted. I don't think I am suited for a life of clerk on the docks of New York."

"Then I'd advise you to forget about your idea," Amy said.

"Well, your advice is good. I'll ruminate on it."

"While you're ruminating, would you like another payment on my debt?"

"Of course," he said, reaching for her and bending down to her lips.

"That was great," she said, "I would like to continue tonight after we've had a delightful dinner and I can slip into something more fitting for debt payment."

Amy surprised Derek by preparing a dish of curried lamb Indian style.

"Where did you learn to cook Indian dishes?" he asked, "you're a lady of many talents. I don't think I've ever told you but there is Indian in my background."

"I read it in one of your earlier bios. One of the ladies in my office is from Mumbai and she taught me. That's the only dish I know, but I might prevail on her to teach me more. Wait here I have another surprise for you." She disappeared into the bedroom and emerged dressed in a bright red sari which showed off a portion of her midriff. Derek gazed at her and felt his body responding to the vibes she was giving off.

"I'm sure none of my ancestors looked like that," he said.

"Am I giving you ideas?" she asked.

"Oh yeah," he replied as he picked her up and carried her into the bedroom,

END

www.ingramcontent.com/pod-product-compliance
Lightning Source LLC
Chambersburg PA
CBHW050544160726
48003CB00002B/739